Almost Perfect

Delia Franklin

BLP

Brick Lane Publishing

First published 2014 in the UK by

Brick Lane Publishing Limited

www.bricklanepublishing.com

1

ISBN: 978-0-9928863-0-1

Cover design: Mary Woolley, Black Flower Creative

In remembrance of the late Boots, my companion as I wrote this. I miss you.

And to those who truly believed in me—you know who you are—thank you for your support.

Chapter One.

GLORIA HYTHE SURVEYED the vegetable patch with hungry, faded-blue eyes. It pleased her that those pesky slugs had been kept at bay by her concoction of crushed eggshells and charcoal scattered around the plants. She eyed the greying sky. It would soon hose down—best gather some lettuce now. She fancied a salad for dinner, along with a thick slice of home-made bread and freshly-made tomato relish, topped with a thick wedge of cheddar. A slice of carrot cake might be quite nice for afterwards, she thought. Her mouth watered at the prospect of all the culinary treats awaiting her.

Off in the distance, a tractor rattled along the rough farm road leading to the house. A dog barked. Then old Will Fox and his big green tractor appeared from behind some trees. A little dog was perched on his knee. The large machine clattered to a halt and the brown and white terrier leapt to the ground. An excited blur of fur whipped around Gloria's legs.

Will climbed gingerly from the tractor. His expression was grim and his silver hair windswept.

'What is it?' asked Gloria. She regarded him as more of a friend than an employer.

With his big hands he fished a small mobile phone from his pocket. Gloria eyed it with some suspicion.

'Lucy,' he said, voice quivering. 'She's had a bad fall from her pony and is in hospital in London. Holly's with her. I'll be off there in a minute myself.'

Lucy was Will's only grandchild and Holly was his only child. His wife had died a couple of years earlier. His only other close relative was a brother who lived in Florida and with whom he seldom spoke.

GLORIA RECKONED SHE could predict Will's moods better than he. When he was upset his brow was furrowed, which reminded her of ploughed fields. The death of his wife, Rosalind—also Gloria's friend—had softened his sometimes rough edges. She recalled his descent into a prickly shell when Rosalind had lost her battle with cancer. At that time he'd shunned proper eating habits and even disappeared at one point for twenty-four hours, giving no indication of his whereabouts. She'd imagined he had drunkenly tumbled into some remote hollow on the farm, was injured and unable to seek help. The howling wind and sheets of rain had only added to her worries.

Upon his whiskey-addled and dishevelled reappearance, Gloria had wisely managed, somewhat, to keep her thoughts to herself. Will was not normally a drunk. In fact, he viewed it akin to weakness of character. But Gloria had understood that he was grieving for his wife. Rosalind's energy and friendship was missed by all and Gloria especially missed their chats. As the weeks ticked by and Will's inebriation had continued, she decided that intervention was necessary to preserve his good health and her peace of mind. She did not want to lose her job, but she also felt some sense of responsibility for Will. So she'd bought a squirming Jack Russell puppy from a local farm.

Two days later and shortly after arriving for her usual housekeeping duties in the morning, she'd presented the pup to Will, saying it needed a good home and that he had plenty of space for a dog on the farm. She'd watched anxiously as he contemplated the tiny creature wriggling in his work-calloused hands. He had gently touched one of the puppy's floppy ears.

'Thank you, Gloria,' he'd whispered eventually, looking

at her with sad, bloodshot eyes. Little white rows of needles gnawed at his grubby thumb. 'I don't really need a dog, but he might be of some use around here. I hope you didn't go to any trouble?'

'Not at all,' she'd replied. 'What will you call him?'

He'd considered this for a moment. 'Sarge,' he'd said. His watery eyes had appeared to spark with tired pleasure, as he thoughtfully rubbed his rough, whiskery chin. 'I've always had that in mind as a good name for a dog.'

'Well, I hope you like him. I'm sure he'll do you proud.'

Sarge had wagged his tail, which was like a tiny aerial, and gazed up at Will.

From that day on, dog and master were inseparable and Will eased off the whisky, much to Gloria's relief.

SARGE SNIFFED AT Gloria's sturdy shoes as she snapped back to reality. She patted Sarge on the rump and drew a deep breath.

'Is Lucy okay?' she ventured anxiously.

Will explained that Lucy's spine was fractured and that she had suffered a serious blow to the head.

Gloria turned away and dabbed her eyes on a clean corner of her apron. 'How dreadful!' she said, her normally clear voice muffled by the cloth. 'Who is there with the child?'

'Just Holly,' he said, a hint of annoyance in his voice. 'Gilbert's on his way back from somewhere or another.'

Gloria's stomach clenched. Thinking fast she said, 'Let's go inside. I'll make a pot of strong tea and we'll think of a way to get you there, right away.' It began to drizzle.

Neither of them had any transport that day. Will's reliable Volvo was having its clutch repaired and Gloria was without her trusty Volkswagen. It had been lent to her niece who was visiting a friend in the next village. She was staying with Gloria to escape her noisy London student flat and study for her dentistry exams. The spare bedroom

3

had become a tangle of clothing, shoes and cosmetics, and so Gloria figured the best thing to do was keep the door firmly closed and avoid the offending sight altogether. Being the gentle soul she was, Gloria reminded herself that she, too, was young once.

Will followed her into the homely kitchen, with Sarge barely half a step behind. Sarge was allowed inside, but only on the wooden floors, which included kitchen, hallway, bathroom and laundry. Will believed that animals belonged outside. Gloria never once mentioned the dog hair on the carpet at the foot of Will's bed. That remained a secret between her and the vacuum cleaner.

Wasting no time, she brewed the strongest pot of tea imaginable. She spooned sugar into both cups. Hot, sweet tea was a trusty panacea. Teacup rattled against saucer as she placed it on the starched, plum-patterned tablecloth. She couldn't stop thinking about Lucy in hospital. And poor Holly, she must be frantic with worry.

They sipped in silence, momentarily sharing an unwelcome sensation of helplessness due to their lack of transport. Sarge sat in front of the range, which was still warm from Gloria's earlier cooking marathon. His alert brown eyes were fixed on his master's lined face.

Will suddenly slapped his knees. 'My tractor!' he exclaimed. 'It will get me to the train station.'

'But Will,' Gloria objected. 'It's four miles away! Besides, where will you park once you get there?'

Will's spirits were by now picking up. He considered Gloria's words for a second and then drained his cup. 'I'll find somewhere.' Glancing at his wristwatch, he stood up. So did Sarge. 'I must go, Gloria. Thanks for the cuppa.'

'Would you like me to rustle up a sandwich to take?'

Gloria also stood and smoothed her apron. She understood immediately that there would be no stopping Will once his mind was made up.

'No thanks,' he replied, briefly nodding at her and moving towards the door. 'Come, Sarge.'

She watched him stride off, Sarge trotting in tow. Taking a few steps after them she called out, 'You can't take animals into hospital and you should change your footwear!'

'I'll be fine,' Will replied over his shoulder. 'Thanks.'

Very soon Will was seated on the tractor with Sarge on his knee. Its engine rattled to life and soon enough the pair lurched away. At the end of the driveway the great machine turned swiftly onto the road and roared ahead at full speed as the drizzle set in.

Gloria listened as the noise of the tractor engine faded from earshot. Returning indoors she noticed with dismay that Will's well-worn wallet was sitting on the table.

FOUR MILES LATER, the noisy tractor rattled conspicuously into the train station car park where a young couple unashamedly stared at him as they drove off. He didn't care; their departure had rather conveniently opened up a parking spot just large enough for the tractor.

He and Sarge made their way into the small station. At the booth Will very nearly asked the attendant for two tickets, one for him and another for Sarge. He paid with a screwed up banknote from his pocket. His wallet was nowhere to be found. He resolved to search his pockets later; at the moment he had a train to catch.

The train trundled to the platform, and with a hiss and a bang, its doors slid open. The stale-smelling carriage was empty, but Will chose the most discreet seat available and the pair settled in for the journey. Sarge lay on the floor for a while, but quickly decided his master's knee was better. From there, he could peer out the window and catch the occasional pat. Swaying swiftly down metal tracks, which weaved by turns through fields and towns, the train drew ever closer to London and its endless buildings.

After what seemed like an eternity, the train squealed into Waterloo Station. What a different scene it was compared with the one they had left in Surrey! Gripping

Sarge's collar, Will took a moment to survey his busy surroundings. Suited and booted men and women constantly checked their phones as they raced about their business. Others clung grimly to handbags and briefcases as they darted in all directions. Tourists lingered with bulging suitcases, staring up at automated timetables that were displayed at a great height for all to see. Will thought it all seemed a bit chaotic.

He scooped Sarge up into his arms and moved out of the way. As he placed Sarge down on the concrete station floor, he noticed for the first time his feet were still in their grubby Wellingtons.

'That woman is always right,' he muttered wryly, thinking of Gloria. Rummaging through pockets for loose change, Will discovered a squashed handkerchief, his mobile phone, a pencil stub, a £10 note and a piece of paper with a scribbled address for the hospital. He realised he must have left his wallet on the kitchen table when he wrote down the hospital's address, and the £10 note was unlikely to be enough for a cab fare there. Taking a ride on the underground was his only option.

Hoisting Sarge into his arms, Will made his way to the underground area. When his turn came to buy a ticket from the machine, he fumbled momentarily and felt a bit foolish before realising that he was required to touch the glass screen for a response. He eventually figured out how everything worked, but not before the queue behind him shuffled with impatience. Finally the machine spat out a ticket, along with a few coins in change.

Locating the correct tube line could be a challenge for the inexperienced traveller. Four different lines passed through Waterloo station and Will had to work out whether his platform was northbound, southbound, eastbound or westbound. Soon he was waiting on the crowded, stuffy platform for the northbound Northern Line with Sarge still in his arms. Presently the tube rattled to a halt and its doors clattered open. The crowds elbowed their way inside. Will sprang into action, somehow managing to squeeze into the last vacant seat. Sarge settled on his master's knee. Both were acutely aware that they must have been an unusual sight.

A well-dressed young woman eyed dog and master with amusement, then nudged her tall, male companion and whispered something to him. Sarge and Will sat swaying as the tube raced through the dark tunnel. Sarge's head hung down, humbly, as if trying not to attract attention. He clearly loved his master. Will sat bolt upright in his muddy Wellingtons, wearing a stubbly frown that said, 'What are you gawping at?'

AT THE HOSPITAL, Sarge had to remain outside. In his haste Will had forgotten to bring something to tie him up with. Just to one side of the hospital's main entrance, he gave Sarge instructions, 'Sit, stay.'

Being an obedient dog, Will knew Sarge would not be distracted by curious, patting strangers. However, as an extra precaution he asked the disinterested hospital security guard to keep an eye on him. To his surprise, the guard said that he would try.

Inside the hospital, memories of his late wife, Rosalind momentarily flashed back. His breath caught in his throat. The hospital environment reminded him of the horrors of Rosalind's chemotherapy. Eventually he found the Intensive Care Unit, also known as the ICU. Instantly his eyes fell on Lucy and he was shocked by the sight of her dear little face, which was almost as white as the sheets she lay on. She looked fragile, was heavily bandaged with tubes sprouting from her nose and mouth, and was connected to some kind of machine that made an artificial breathing noise. A nurse hovered discreetly to one side of the bed and was deftly tapping something into a computer.

His only child, Holly, had been in the ward for hours, anxiously watching over Lucy. She was pacing the floor with a determinedly brave face. Will knew that expression; he had seen it before. Father and daughter embraced.

'Dad, I'm scared,' whispered Holly. His familiar smell of Pears soap and farm was comforting to her.

'Lucy's a fighter,' Will said gruffly, not sure of what else to say. He saw the fear in Holly's toffee-coloured eyes as he drew away. 'What are the doctors saying?'

'Fortunately her spinal cord is undamaged,' Holly replied. She eyed his Wellingtons. 'But they have done further tests.'

'For what?' Will asked, taking a step back.

Holly was silent.

'For what?' he repeated, more urgently.

'Possible brain damage,' she said softly, meeting his gaze. 'Lucy took a nasty knock when she fell from her pony. They've put her in a temporary, medically-induced coma to preserve higher brain functions.'

Will turned away to compose himself. He struggled to stem his tears as the shock of this news engulfed him. He was of the old school and didn't like to show emotion.

Welcoming a change of subject an amused smile seized the corners of Holly's mouth. 'You dropped everything to get here didn't you, Dad! How did you do it?'

'Tractor, train and tube.' He replied in a matter of fact tone, still turned away from his daughter. 'Sarge is outside by the hospital entrance.'

'I'll go and see him. I need a cigarette. Care to join me?'

Will declined. He needed to take stock of Lucy's condition.

'Do you mind if I pop out for a moment?'

Of course he didn't. As Holly traipsed outside, Will seated himself by Lucy's bed.

'Lucy,' he whispered. 'It's your old granddad.' He tenderly touched her cheek; if there was any kind of response it was imperceptible.

Soon a doctor approached. The young man introduced himself as Dr Roberts and they shook hands.

'William Fox, the lass's granddad.'

'Pleased to meet you,' Dr Roberts said. 'I have some news. Is Lucy's mother far away?'

'Outside for a breath of fresh air,' Will replied. 'She'll only be a few minutes—is it urgent? I can fetch her.'

Scratching his head, Will hoped desperately for some good news. He sat down creakily. He would not know what to do should the news be bad.

Dr Roberts quickly identified the old man's feelings.

'Mr Fox, it's nothing to worry about.' He gave a comforting smile and ran a hand through his blond, overgrown hair. 'I'll pop back in ten minutes with details.'

'Call me Will.'

Dr Roberts had seen Will's expression many times before. He understood people's pain. Dealing with all kinds of physical and emotional suffering was part of the job. Observing the Wellingtons, farm attire and grim expression, he sensed a good man in Will. With a sympathetic nod, he turned and left the room.

Will went to the window. Outside this sterile hospital room, life carried on. Trees swayed in the wind and as far as the eye could see, was brick, concrete and glass. He stood for a moment hoping Lucy would be okay, and was still there when Holly swished back into the room, her long russet-brown hair ruffled by the wind. She smelled of cigarettes and freshly applied perfume.

She sat by Lucy's bed and touched her daughter's hand. Will saw the worry etched on Holly's brow and the tension in her shoulders. They were silent until Dr Roberts appeared at the doorway a few moments later.

'Hello again,' he said. His tone was upbeat.

Returning his greeting, Will heard his daughter inhale sharply.

Dr Roberts cleared his throat.

'I won't waste any time telling you. The MRI scan results we took earlier show some encouraging signs, but we will need to closely monitor her brain swelling.'

9

He paused, and then continued. 'Lucy obviously took quite a blow to the head when she came off her horse. I'd like to keep her in the coma and lower her body temperature for a week or so, to reduce any brain swelling.'

Will nodded, and Dr Roberts shifted on his feet.

'Her spinal cord is completely undamaged, so that's good news,' Dr Roberts said. He offered a generous smile, more than the usual tight-lipped version offered by doctors in general. 'You should try getting a good sleep tonight. We're looking after her.'

Somehow Dr Roberts did not think either of the pair standing before him would sleep particularly well. 'The best thing you can do right now is try not to worry.'

He eyed Will's Wellingtons again.

'Quick trip into town was it, Will?'

'Aye. She's my only grandchild.'

Will found himself frowning at Dr Roberts without meaning to. Holly's hand tightened on her father's arm. She smiled reassuringly at the doctor.

'Thanks for the update, Dr Roberts,' she spoke carefully. 'That's, uh—' she paused, searching for the right words. 'That's encouraging news.'

Holly contemplated her next question. 'How long will it take for Lucy to, you know, return…to normal?' She rushed the last two words out.

'It can take a few months for everything to fully heal, but the worst will hopefully be over in a few weeks.' Dr Roberts had stated the facts, but decided to qualify them. 'Some people take longer to recover than others. Fortunately she's young and healthy and hopefully there won't be any complications. But she will need to take it easy. No horse riding for a long time.'

Dr Roberts cleared his throat and continued. 'Sometimes people forget what happened. But it's not something to be overly alarmed about in the bigger scheme of things.' Pausing, he asked, 'Was there anything else you wanted to discuss right now?'

Father and daughter glanced at each other.

'I think we understand,' Holly replied. 'Thank you.'

Dr Roberts smiled and Holly noticed his kindly, flint-grey eyes. Will shook his hand.

'If you need anything at all, please use the buzzer. I'll also check in periodically before the end of my shift and there will always be a nurse present, too. Take care.' With that, Dr Roberts slipped out.

'Dad...' Holly's eyes welled with tears.

Will hugged her. 'Lucy's a fighter, like her mum and old granddad, too,' he said.

Will excused himself momentarily to check on Sarge. He was greeted with enthusiastic tail wagging and hand licking while the hospital security guard looked on.

'Your dog hasn't budged an inch,' he said approvingly.

Will gave Sarge an extra pat. Sometimes he wondered if the little dog sensed his moods. He glanced at his wristwatch and realised it was probably time to head back home. He would return tomorrow.

After phoning Gloria with the news—she wouldn't forgive him if he neglected to do so—he made his way back to the ward to say goodbye to Holly and deliver strict instructions for her to contact him should there be any change in Lucy's condition, no matter the time.

'Dad, stop fussing, you heard the doctor. Try not to worry.' Holly squeezed her father's shoulder affectionately. She was glad to see him. Having him around had made the situation with Lucy more bearable. 'And leave your tractor at home when you come back tomorrow,' she added with a wry smile.

Chapter Two.

AFTER A FEW hours Holly relinquished her bedside vigil over seven-year-old Lucy. She was as satisfied as she could be given the circumstances, and decided to drive home and try for a full night's sleep. She resolved to return to the hospital and Lucy early the next morning.

After locking the heavy, familiar front door of her house behind her Holly shrugged off her overcoat and with an audible sigh, stepped out of her uncomfortable shoes, which had been pinching her swollen feet all day. She enjoyed the cool, tiled marble surface beneath her stocking-clad toes. She left her overcoat and shoes for Iris, the housekeeper, to pick up.

Holly's dog, Spock, sleepily padded over to greet her and solicit a pat. Her husband, Gilbert, was at this moment winging his way back to Heathrow from New York. On hearing the news of Lucy's accident he had booked the next flight home and cancelled his business meetings.

Gilbert was due to land early tomorrow morning. Holly expected he would hang around for a few obligatory days and then return to New York and his unfinished business there. She trudged upstairs and into the large master bedroom, which was filled mainly with her things and only a few traces of Gilbert's.

Gilbert loved Holly and Lucy, but in practical terms was virtually uninvolved in their lives. It was Holly who went to the parent-teacher meetings at school and took Lucy to ballet classes twice a week. It was Holly who

12

clapped and cheered when Lucy was the Sugar Plum Fairy at the ballet academy's annual Christmas performance of the *Nutcracker*. She'd fought terribly with Gilbert over his non-attendance. Making time for such occasions was important, Holly reckoned, and surely his meetings could be side-lined from time to time?

LUCY WAS REMARKABLY attuned to the subtle moods and swirling undercurrents of adult subtext, and knew to slip quietly from a room when an argument between her parents was brewing. She knew to squeeze her granddad's rough farmer's hand with her little plump one when he was thinking of Rosalind. Lucy was cool, self-contained and wise beyond her years. During class break at school she sought the company of older girls, who liked plaiting her long and smooth blond hair.

Holly was passionate and sensitive. Above all, she was a devoted mother. Mostly it was just the pair of them at home in the enormous, ten-bedroom country house, along with Iris. There was also Michael, the caretaker, who spent a lot of time at Larkspur, tending to its glasshouses and gardens, set on eight acres of land. Holly and Lucy loved Larkspur, which was close enough to the attractions of London and yet suitably distant from its ceaseless crowds.

On the odd occasion when Gilbert was around he somewhat guiltily made up for his absences by buying Lucy all of the things a young girl could wish for: pretty clothes, shoes, sparkly baubles with real gemstones and a pony. In fact, it was *that* pony she fell from.

Holly sighed as she crawled into bed and arranged the pillows. She'd objected when the pony arrived for Lucy's seventh birthday, saying Lucy was too young for such things. She didn't want their daughter to become spoiled.

Gilbert also lavished Holly with gifts. Rare black pearls, more diamond jewellery than she knew what to do with, perfume, designer handbags, lingerie and various other things women in their twenties ordinarily loved to own.

One thing that could be said in favour of Gilbert was his uncanny knack for buying that perfect gift.

On the occasions when Gilbert was home, the couple rowed frequently, and often in quite a heated manner. Occasionally, she even lost her temper with him. Holly's frustration festered, and she began to question whether or not she was driving Gilbert from Larkspur.

'All I want is my husband!' she once roared, flinging a pair of Manolo Blahnic shoes rather ungratefully against the wall. 'I feel like a bloody single mother!'

It seemed the only thing that Gilbert's hefty income couldn't afford was time with his attention-starved family. Investment banking demanded all of his available time, and then some, and he all too readily accepted its terms. By popular convention, investment bankers were known to be self-absorbed. Perhaps their belief that they were somewhat superior to other mortal beings was linked to the multi-million-pound deals they brokered.

Born into the old and established Tatton family, Gilbert grew up in the middle of nowhere with pedigree and connections, but a shortage of liquid cash. Cracked portraits of long-dead ancestors had adorned the walls of his childhood home, and threadbare Persian rugs had covered the creaking floorboards. His father had run a moderately successful local law firm. He'd earned enough money to support his family and pay for his children's private education, but not quite enough for the adequate upkeep of their estate. Proper maintenance and repair had generally been avoided and many of the home's draughty rooms had been sealed to keep gas and electricity costs down. Only the immediate living areas had been heated, and then always by a traditional wood fire.

To keep a further lid on bills, housework and gardening duties had been divided among the family. The ancient caretaker—whose family had been caretakers of the estate for generations—had never seemed to accomplish much and nobody had had the heart to move him on.

Gilbert and his sister Fiona had been forced to lend a hand whenever they were home from boarding school. Gilbert had had to chop and stack firewood, rake leaves, clear snow off paths, mow lawns and clean windows. He'd hated these tasks and had seen them as demeaning. Fiona had learned to cook and clean from a young age. They had never discussed their situation while growing up and were not particularly close.

Gilbert had always been envious of his classmates who appeared to be wealthier than he. To avoid embarrassment he'd never invited friends back to his family home on weekends or during his school holidays. He had instead visited their immaculate homes, and invariably compared his humiliatingly humble existence with their abundant living conditions. Gilbert had grown up with memories of not much play and of winter being perpetually smoky, chilly and damp. He'd looked forward to summer with great eagerness because life generally became a lot more comfortable, and he'd spent most of his time outdoors and out of earshot.

When the time came, Gilbert had chosen his future profession based solely on earning potential. It had been only a matter of time before his school connections secured him a job at a private American investment bank in London's famous square-mile business district. Potential customers were required to be high net-worth individuals, which was a polite way of saying they were filthy rich. Gilbert had immediately set about restoring his pride by becoming wealthy in his own right. His first ever Christmas bonus had been sixty-five thousand pounds, more than enough for a deposit on a reasonable house.

'It's been a tough year,' his boss had apologised. 'I'm sorry your bonus is so small.'

With his bonus and some extra savings he had accrued, Gilbert had paid a deposit on Larkspur, which was in Guilford, Surrey, and was a nascent enclave for wealthy, commuting Londoners. His job had been going well, so he'd employed a fulltime housekeeper and a caretaker to keep his estate pristine. Every room in the house was perfectly kept and it delighted him to stroll from room to room and gloat.

The booming global economy had seen Gilbert's bonuses and salary increase significantly. Earning decidedly more than his school chums pleased Gilbert a great deal. In fact, he'd begun receiving regular bonuses well in excess of two hundred thousand pounds, sometimes even more. Soon, his colleagues had been indulging in flashy lads' nights out, splashing their cash at swanky clubs on ostentatious Cristal Methuselah champagne bottles, worth a wipe-out twenty thousand pounds each to less wealthy individuals. Gilbert had gone out a couple of times with his colleagues, but their sleazy excesses had disgusted him. Besides, he'd still had a mortgage to pay off. And so Gilbert had been careful to squirrel away his earnings. It had been around this time that he met Holly.

THE ANNUAL SUMMER Cricket Ball coincided with a beautiful, balmy summer evening. Holly was best friends with Tammy Cunningham, and Gilbert was the private-client banker to her parents. The Cunningham family hosted the ball every year and eighteen-year-old Holly was invited as Tammy's guest.

Holly looked stunning. Her russet brown hair was swept up into a messy knot and decorated with small white rosebuds, which had the effect of crowning her lithe body, swathed in a smoky pink silk dress. As she laughed unselfconsciously with her friends, she briefly caught Gilbert's eye. He watched from across the room as a slightly gangly and floppy haired young man led her onto the dance floor.

Gilbert had grown bored of the ever-present and over-primped gold diggers that his line of work attracted. The girls knew exactly where wealthy bankers ate, drank and even exercised. Everywhere he went, they went too. At first they'd been an easy bit of fun. However, their manicured nails, perma-tans, perfect hair, fake breasts and shallow conversation eventually felt pointless, stupid and utterly predictable.

By contrast, Holly's beauty was natural and wholesome. She had an oval face, high cheekbones, a generous smile and a neat nose sprinkled with a few summer freckles. Gilbert found himself alongside the couple on the dance floor. She smelled faintly of coconut.

'May I cut in?' His heart thumped loudly as he looked in fascination at the radiant girl in front of him. Blimey, he hadn't realised she was quite so young—early twenties, perhaps?

'Sorry,' Holly replied, looking away.

Gilbert was thrown off guard. The last thing he'd expected was to be brushed off. He didn't realise Holly was actually apologising to her dance partner, who did a poor job of hiding his annoyance at being cut out.

Much to Gilbert's surprise she turned to him and grasped his still outstretched hand. Regaining his composure, he steered her across the dance floor. The floppy-haired young man slunk off to chew canapés and glower at the pair from a distance for a little while.

'Pleased to meet you. I'm Gilbert.' Investment banking had taught him to remain calm and collected, even when he felt the opposite.

'I'm Holly.' She gazed mischievously at him. 'Thanks for cutting in. He had really sweaty palms.'

'You're welcome.' Gilbert smiled at her. Holly noticed that his eyes were a nice blue-green colour.

As they waltzed, Holly was oblivious to the many pairs of admiring male eyes flitting in her direction. Gilbert, on the other hand, wasn't and pulled Holly ever so slightly closer to send the signal she was his for now, but not so close as to alarm her. One dance followed another as the loveliness of the starry summer night cast its spell. The champagne and moonlit country setting added to the magic, and the pair basked in the first glow of mutual fascination. In fact, many a face turned and gazed at them with admiration.

As the evening drew to a close Gilbert was certain he wanted to see Holly again.

'I'm taking my new car for a spin around the countryside tomorrow afternoon,' he ventured as she escorted him to a pre-ordered taxi. 'Would you like to come out with me for a drive?'

Holly pondered momentarily. Wasn't Gilbert, well, a bit *old* to be interested in her? On the other hand, she'd had a wonderful time dancing with him. He was attentive, but not overly so, amusing and altogether charming. His classically handsome looks also appealed to her. Feeling flattered she replied with a giggle, 'I will if you don't ask me to wash the windscreen afterwards!'

EARLY THE NEXT morning and with a spring in his step Gilbert asked his trusty housekeeper to pack a picnic lunch for two. With raised eyebrows, Iris set off to the village to fetch supplies. She privately held the view that Gilbert was in dire need of some decent, feminine company. She presented him with a tasty hamper he could be proud of, containing fresh bread, ham from the bone, a variety of cheeses, Belgian chocolates and fresh fruit. She also slipped in a cheeky bottle of champagne and some seasonal berries soaked in vodka—a heady combination.

It was midday when Gilbert collected Holly from Tammy's home. The girls were hugely impressed with Gilbert's car. Holly felt grown up as Gilbert opened the passenger's door for her. She liked the way his blonde hair was slightly longer on top, and his chinos and rugby sweater showed off his broad shoulders.

The growling Aston Martin engine transported Holly into the pretty depths of Surrey's leafy countryside. Gilbert had done his homework and located a suitable picnic spot in a sunny meadow off a winding country lane. The scenery and heady summer air were intoxicating, not to mention the champagne, Holly thought as she sipped the velvety liquid and giggled at something amusing that Gilbert was saying.

This was the perfect date, she thought, remembering some awful ones she had experienced with boys who had not known quite how to act around her. Some had tried too hard to impress, while others feigned indifference. It never occurred to Holly that they might be intimidated by her unselfconscious good looks. Her worst date had been with the neighbour's son. Inviting her to a rugby match at Twickenham, after one too many beers and a Cornish pasty, he'd tried groping her on the train home, his attempts reminding her of someone getting gherkins from a jar with oven mitts. Mortified, Holly had moved to a different seat for the remaining journey, while her date sulked.

'Sounds like *my* perfect date!' Tammy had laughed when Holly told her about it afterwards.

On the other hand, her picnic with Gilbert was divine. Receiving the attention of a sophisticated, handsome man, who knew exactly how to behave, was undeniably flattering. Holly was impressed and smitten.

WHEN HOLLY RETURNED home to her parents, she told them about her date with Gilbert and assured them of his gentlemanly behaviour. Somewhat predictably they did not share Holly's enthusiasm and privately thought he was too old for their daughter. Knowing how stubborn young Holly could be when the mood took her, they grudgingly accepted she was old enough to make her own decisions.

When they met Gilbert, his impeccable manners and affable demeanour won them over, but not entirely so. They were counting on the whole thing being a romantic fling that would fizzle out in short order.

Holly's close friendship with Tammy was side-lined when Tammy flew to the other side of the world for her gap year. She would spend one month in Thailand, five months in New Zealand and then six months in Australia. The girls kept in touch, giggling for hours into the phone. Holly whispered details of the latest restaurant or theatre performance she had attended with Gilbert. Tammy loved to hear every detail of her friend's romance, although she, too, thought Gilbert was a bit old for Holly.

'Have you done it yet?' she asked Holly directly.

'Done what? If you mean kissed—then yes.' Gilbert was a marvellous kisser and Holly tingled all over just thinking about it.

Tammy could scarcely believe that her best friend hadn't yet slept with Gilbert. Holly was an old-fashioned romantic who had decided to wait for the right moment in time, and ideally that would be the night of her wedding.

'Why wait?' Tammy said, meanwhile having plenty of fun with antipodean men. She described them with relish, regaling Holly with all the details of her latest exploit. Holly shrieked with laughter and remarked how tame her love life was in comparison. On reflection, she decided that she wouldn't trade her romance with Gilbert for Tammy's torrid flings for one second.

Back at Larkspur, Gilbert whistled as he dressed after swimming forty lengths of his heated indoor pool.

'At last, Gilbert is finding time to enjoy all of his money,' Iris whispered to Michael, the caretaker.

Michael was a quiet man who couldn't care less about Gilbert's love life, much less whether his own socks matched. He wasn't interested in Iris's gossip, either. The pair had a tenuous relationship, but he listened with half an ear to her chatter as she busily snipped rose blooms from his beloved glasshouses to adorn Larkspur's many rooms.

THREE MONTHS INTO their blossoming relationship, Holly boarded an airplane with her parents and flew to Malta for a three-week holiday. They were hoping she would forget about Gilbert.

Gilbert found himself in a curious situation. He was tormented by jealousy as he pictured muscular men in swimming trunks chatting smoothly to his girlfriend on the beach.

Is this—love? Gilbert asked himself, tossing and turning in his bed and unable to sleep.

Following several days and nights of serious soul-searching, Gilbert took the bull by the horns and resolved to propose to Holly shortly after her return. He would ask the question while the pair floated elegantly above Larkspur in a hot air balloon with a wicker basket.

Gilbert wasted no time in consulting the weather maps to be sure his grand plans wouldn't be spoiled by rain. He mentioned the planned expedition to Iris, but omitted his intention to propose. She somewhat predictably offered to pack a picnic hamper; she loved feeding people.

'Thank you, Iris,' Gilbert said, knowing without question how good it would be. Then he contacted Holly and let her know he had a surprise outing planned for the following Saturday.

Holly was excited at the prospect of seeing Gilbert again and looked forward to the outing. Malta had been wonderful, but she missed Gilbert's calm sense of fun.

Saturday arrived and he drove her to a nearby meadow where the hot air balloon was waiting. She had never been in a balloon before. Up close it was far bigger than the ones she had seen in the skies previously. They climbed into the basket, and before long they were sailing into the afternoon sky, the fields below soon taking on the appearance of an extensive patchwork quilt.

Gilbert proposed high above the Surrey countryside in the warm afternoon air.

Holly was lost for words. Obviously they had been spending a lot of time together, but she'd never expected this. Being a dyed-in-the-wool romantic, she had imagined her father's permission would be sought first, followed by a proposal and then together they would choose the ring.

Gilbert produced a small red box and opened it. Inside, a ring with three large, princess cut diamonds sparkled as it caught the afternoon rays. It was stunning and no doubt extremely expensive.

'Cartier,' he said hopefully, heart in his mouth.

Holly looked at the stunning ring then into his earnest blue-green eyes. She took a deep breath.

'Yes,' she accepted at last. She loved Gilbert and was dazzled by the brilliant ring. It was a fairytale!

Gilbert felt a mixture of joy and relief. He hugged Holly so tight that she almost stopped breathing.

'Gilbert!' she squeaked in protest.

He could feel her heart thumping beneath her breasts. Pulling away a little, he said, 'I was thinking we could get married sooner rather than later. What do you think?'

Holly was breathless. 'How soon?'

'Six months?' He had respected her decision to wait until marriage before consummating their relationship, but now, all of a sudden, he found it so very difficult to wait. She was a beautiful and desirable young woman. Better still, she didn't know it. She was perfect!

'Gilbert!' Holly squeaked again. 'So soon! Who will help us?'

'My mother, your mother, Iris, probably.' He inhaled the clean, coconut aroma of her hair, quite overcome with happiness.

Holly had met the frosty and formidable Mrs Tatton once before and was not altogether sure that she liked her. She reminded Holly of someone who had taken a deep breath long ago and then forgotten to exhale. Her face might crack if she ever volunteered anything more than a stiff smile. Holly almost giggled at the idea.

She imagined her own mother would be happy to help. But what would Dad say? She imagined he would say she was too young, advise her to go to university and then see how she felt about Gilbert afterwards. She knew they would protest, but was so happy that she didn't care. She loved Gilbert, and would convince her parents. Besides, nineteen was a suitably grown up age!

GILBERT DECIDED TO break the news of their engagement to Holly's parents at lunch the next day. He reserved a table at a suitably swanky, yet discreet, London restaurant.

Will almost choked on his salmon starter when he heard the news. Rosalind was shocked, but diplomatic. She put down her cutlery and congratulated the beaming couple. She and Will liked Gilbert, but they were worried about the age gap. He was decent, affable and seemed devoted to their daughter. Yet, Rosalind had her doubts. To begin with, it was all very sudden. Then there was the eleven-year age gap to consider and Holly had not yet begun university. In fact, they were increasingly doubtful she would enrol at all. Based on recent comments it seemed Holly planned on going to art school instead; she was clever with a brush and canvas.

An awkward silence fell over the table. Gilbert managed to look both a jot worried and bored all at once, his eyes wandering to his spoon and cup, then to Holly who was twisting the sparkling ring on her finger. They sat for what seemed like an eternity until Rosalind spoke. She took Gilbert's hand, squeezed it and smiled at him with blue eyes that were simultaneously kind and steely.

'Just make sure you look after her. She's our only child and we love her a great deal,' she said.

'Mum.' Holly looked embarrassed.

'I've got a right to speak my mind and I will,' Rosalind said, still squeezing Gilbert's hand. 'You're our little girl and we don't want you changing into another person altogether. We raised you and we want nothing but your happiness. If happiness means marrying Gilbert, then you have our blessing. But perhaps waiting a little longer wouldn't hurt.'

'I don't want to wait,' Holly protested.

Gilbert no longer looked relaxed. He gazed intently at Rosalind, who sighed and contemplated what to say next.

'If it means you're happy, who are we to stop you? But you need to think about what sort of person you want to be. In ten years' time you'll have changed, and what you want now you may no longer want then.' She took a breath. 'And what about university?'

Holly glanced at Gilbert before she spoke.

'Well, it kind of makes sense to hold off doing anything for six months with the wedding coming up and all that.'

Before Rosalind could reply, Will leaned over and hugged Holly. She was his little girl, and it seemed like just yesterday she was making daisy chains and feeding calves from teat-bottles on the farm. He figured she would probably be feeding her own child next. Heaven forbid it should happen too soon! He hoped this wasn't a shotgun wedding.

'I love you, Dad,' she whispered into his shoulder. He smelled like always, of Pears soap and farm.

He hugged her tight. He wanted to say so much, but thought it unwise given his current frame of mind.

Gilbert was politely sitting back as this was happening, waiting for an appropriate moment to speak.

Taking the plunge, he said, 'I appreciate you being good sports about the suddenness of our engagement.' Raising his espresso cup, he continued. 'I realise how precious Holly is to you both, and I can assure you she is also very precious to me. You needn't worry, I will look after her.'

It occurred to Rosalind that the term 'good sport' was not fitting. It was better suited to tennis, or some such lesser matter.

Will extended his hand to Gilbert and gruffly shook it. 'Congratulations. Look after our little girl.'

'I will, Mr Fox,' Gilbert promised. He signalled to the waiter, who was lurking at a discreet distance trying to figure out what the subtext of the conversation meant.

'The bill please,' Gilbert ordered. The waiter scurried off immediately. Turning to Will and Rosalind, Gilbert smiled. 'I'll take care of this,' he said.

It also occurred to Rosalind that Gilbert was very used to getting what he wanted.

HOURS AFTER THEIR lavish London wedding, Gilbert and Holly arrived at a private Maldives honeymoon island. Gilbert wasted no time. He began to remove every last scrap of Holly's clothing until she stood naked and self-conscious in the centre of the room. Admiring her feminine form, he gently picked her up and laid her on the bed. His hands caressed her soft, warm skin until she was languid and relaxed.

'Wait right there,' he said, standing to remove his own clothing.

Holly watched, fascinated. She had never before seen a man naked in the flesh. Gilbert looked like a sculpted Greek statue. His chest was sprinkled with hair and a line of it ran down his belly and disappeared into his pants, which he was now removing. As he stepped out of them and straightened, her eyes were fixed on him. A curious ache stirred within her.

During their two-week honeymoon, they barely left their opulent suite. Gilbert was exceptionally attentive to her every mood, and Holly hadn't been this happy in all of her short life. For the first time, she was madly and deeply in love. He was her first lover, too. The thought of him with other women previously nearly drove her to distraction.

'How many others have you had?' she ventured one day after a particularly long and leisurely morning in bed.

'You're all that counts,' he replied.

Still curious but satisfied enough, Holly accepted his answer, snuggling against his well-shaped chest.

It was a magical time of discovery, where they learned many things about one another. Gilbert disliked cats and chewing gum. His favourite food was chicken parmesan and he loved swimming in the ocean. Holly was terrified of sharks; she hated beetroot and liked cats and dogs equally. She couldn't decide what her favourite food was, but she did confess to an occasional sweet tooth.

One particularly hot afternoon they walked the few steps from their suite and onto the private beach. Gilbert went swimming while Holly watched from the safety of her sun-lounger. After much persuasion Gilbert convinced Holly to try the water, which she bravely did, although not for long. Then she dozed in the shade of their beach umbrella while he swam some more. She awoke to the sensation of dripping water and opened her eyes to find Gilbert standing there, fresh from the ocean and holding a camera.

'Smile!' he said.

She obliged.

Gilbert loved that photo, his favourite honeymoon memory. It brought a smile to his face every time he saw it, and thereafter he carried a copy with him everywhere.

TWO MONTHS AFTER the wedding, Holly and Gilbert had their first disagreement. Holly quickly learned it was Iris and Michael who kept Larkspur running like a well-oiled machine. They argued about Iris and whether her housekeeping hours should be trimmed back. Holly wasn't entirely comfortable with having everything done for her and wanted to prove that she was capable of rolling up her sleeves and dunking her hands into a kitchen sink. Growing up, things had been different with Gloria, the Fox family housekeeper, who liked it when Holly chipped in from time to time and the pair had nattered away. Although Holly liked Iris she found it irritating that she did absolutely everything for her, from making breakfast to buying groceries each week. It made Holly feel cosseted and she didn't like it one bit.

Reducing Iris's working hours seemed the logical

solution to Holly. That way she would feel more like the real mistress of Larkspur. Gilbert disagreed, surmising that she couldn't cope with running such a large house on her own, especially with art school coming up. When Holly suggested closing up some of the unused rooms, she observed a mental switch flick behind Gilbert's eyes. She had never before seen him like that.

Gilbert stubbornly refused Holly's request and insisted the entire house and all of its rooms remain open and maintained at all times. That meant Iris must continue to work fulltime; no amount of persuasion would sway him.

Holly told Gilbert he was being very unreasonable and stormed out to sleep in one of the guest bedrooms.

Halfway through the night he found her. He told her of his youth, and his family home. He told her that despite their family crest and estate, there was never quite enough money. That his family home was only ever half lived in. He recounted every detail right down to the conservatory roof where ugly smears of brown and orange slime had settled due to years of neglect.

Holly listened and wondered what all the fuss was about. He had more than most people, didn't he?

THE NEXT DAY, Holly pulled Iris to one side while she was vacuuming one of the many bedrooms.

'Iris, could I please speak with you for a minute?'

Iris looked surprised and switched off the noisy machine. 'Of course,' she said.

Holly cleared her throat. 'Iris, please don't take this the wrong way, but I feel a bit, er, unhelpful around here because you do everything and I don't lift a finger.'

Iris eyed her carefully. She understood that some women wanted to possess their own domestic kingdom, and in her canny estimation, young Holly fit that criteria. But Iris needed the money to cover her monthly mortgage payments and support her elderly mother. Not missing a beat, she explained her circumstances.

Holly pondered on this. 'Gilbert spends every Wednesday night in London,' she ventured.

'Ah, I see.' Realisation dawned on Iris. She considered what to say next and knew it was probably not going to be too delicate. 'You want me to take the day off without Mr Tatton knowing.'

'Yes, please.'

'That could work, but I don't know how it could be explained to Michael, the caretaker.'

'Could you tell him?' Holly looked slightly desperate.

Iris wasn't entirely comfortable with the arrangement, but she did like the prospect of an extra day off on full pay. She tucked a strand of her short, ash-blonde hair behind her ear. 'I'll see what I can do but if Mr Tatton ever finds out—'

'I'll explain it was my doing entirely.'

'Very well,' Iris said. 'Leave it to me.' She pressed a button on the vacuum cleaner and it whirred back to life.

Whatever Iris said to Michael obviously worked because she didn't appear for work the next Wednesday.

Chapter Three.

HOLLY'S EYES SNAPPED open at 06:00 and for a split second she wondered why her alarm was set so early. Then her brain caught up; it was Wednesday—Iris's newly appointed day off. Holly had pressed her for a list of chores, which turned out to be baking, dusting and vacuuming. It didn't seem like much, but Iris had assured her it was plenty and not to be surprised if she didn't manage to get everything finished in one day.

Holly stumbled barefoot to the kitchen in search of coffee. She had been discreetly observing the numerous duties Iris performed on a daily basis. Yesterday, Iris had rather reluctantly shown Holly where the cleaning products and vacuum cleaner were kept. Iris had privately thought Holly might struggle with the large amount of housework Larkspur required—if she didn't lose interest first. She expected Holly would be the usual rich and entitled type.

After wrestling with getting the grounds into the cappuccino machine, Holly produced a steaming mug of coffee. She stirred in milk and sugar and took a large gulp. She had a positive feeling about today. Gilbert was due home that weekend and she planned to bake his favourite cranberry brownies. She cast about for a recipe book and proceeded to set the oven to the right temperature. She measured out the necessary ingredients including a great deal of butter and sugar. In no time at all she had whipped up an appetizing batter, confirmed with a quick taste test.

Feeling confident, she spread the mixture evenly around the tin and with a satisfied sigh she placed it in the oven. Wiping her hands, she decided to freshen up for the day. After setting the timer for fifteen minutes she strode upstairs.

In the en-suite bathroom and feeling super-efficient, Holly decided to give herself a quick deep conditioning treatment. Keeping one eye on the bathroom clock, Holly massaged the gooey, coconut-scented mixture into her mane and quickly soaped herself down. Once showered, she threw on some jeans and a pink, silk-blend top Gilbert had bought back for her from one of his recent business trips. She scraped her damp hair up into a knot, and to complete her sophisticated housewifely image, spritzed on some perfume. She had quite a collection of bottles, mainly gifts from other people. She settled on one closest to her, a breezy scent with vanilla top notes.

Back in the kitchen, Holly was relieved not to smell burning. She whipped the tray from the oven and winced when she caught her wrist on the edge of the oven door. Something was wrong. The brownies were a little gooey. She gently prodded them and consulted the recipe book, suddenly noticing that the baking time was in fact fifty minutes. Feeling somewhat foolish she put this minor mishap down to the perils of pre-breakfast baking.

After half an hour and some breakfast, the buzzer sounded. This time the brownies were firm to touch with small cracks appearing on the surface. Leaving them to cool, she moved onto her next task, dusting. Gosh, at this rate everything would be in order by lunchtime, she thought. Her wrist throbbed a little where she had caught it earlier and so she ran it under some cold water. Glancing at the clock, Holly decided to make her third coffee of the day, reasoning that in situations where one needed extra energy, such things were necessary.

After downing her brew and with her wrist suitably patched, Holly cast about for dusting cloths—ones with special particle-attracting properties that Iris raved about—which were nowhere to be found. Her eyes fell on a neatly folded stack of tea-towels. Grabbing several, she bounded from the kitchen and began dusting the large marble-tiled reception room, with its various sideboards and cabinets. She polished the carved wooden bannister of the grand staircase leading up to the next floor and its many rooms, which she would get to later. To be honest, everything seemed clean enough already. The trick, she supposed, was to stay on top of things.

In the lounge-room overlooking the expansive garden she selected an upbeat radio station. Turning up the volume, she set to work taking care not to knock any ornaments as she cleaned. Singing loudly, she tried not to think of Larkspur's many rooms awaiting her.

'Ma'am?' a deep voice cut through the lyrics. Holly jumped and in doing so, upended a heavy antique vase—a Waterford and no doubt expensive. In slow motion it toppled from the sideboard and towards the hard parquet floor. With lightning reflexes, Holly caught it in mid-air, placed it carefully on the sideboard and then turned the stereo volume down. Michael stood at the doorway with a basket of freshly cut roses from the glasshouses. His silver-flecked eyebrows were raised in surprise.

'Ma'am—Iris will be back tomorrow?' The sight of Holly cleaning with a tea-towel clearly baffled him.

'That's right.' Holly's face was pink and she hoped Michael wasn't about to start questioning her arrangement with Iris. For a second, she wondered exactly what Iris had said to him, but changed the subject.

'Call me Holly,' she said with a tentative smile. She was not one to embrace airs and graces. She had, after all, been raised on a farm.

Michael warmed to the energetic young woman standing before him with pink painted toenails. He fidgeted with the basket in his hands.

'Where would you like the roses, er…Mrs Tatton?'

31

Holly let it slide. 'In the kitchen would be great.'

He nodded and ambled off.

BY LUNCHTIME HOLLY was tired but determined. Larkspur was dust-free and gleaming. Better still, nothing had been broken.

Holly consulted the list and sipped at her coffee. Next: vacuuming. She inspected the cranberry brownies and decided it would be sensible to sample one or two slices before cutting and putting them away. After gobbling three she jogged from the kitchen in search of the vacuum cleaner and began her task in the lounge-room. Approaching the sideboard somewhat over-zealously, her elbow clipped its edge. Her funny-bone vibrated in protest and she dropped the pipe. Before she could react, the Waterford vase—which she vaguely remembered was a wedding present—toppled and smashed on the floor. Heavy shards whizzed across its wooden surface, settling under sofas and sideboards. Stemming tears, Holly cursed and set out to find a broom and some newspaper.

'Stupid, suicidal vase.' She gulped, hoping Michael wouldn't walk in right then. Unable to find anything to wrap the shards with she swept them into a neat pile under the sideboard. She would come back to it later.

With her energy levels heading for a spectacular post-caffeine slump, she moved upstairs to the next floor, taking extra care to avoid further accidents. Gritting her teeth, Holly vacuumed until she was ready to die of boredom. How Iris did it, day in, day out was beyond her. She finished on the top floor in the master bedroom and by this time, she had well and truly had enough. After stowing the machine in the wardrobe she flopped on the large bed. She would remove the Waterford remains and wash those grubby tea-towels once she was done napping. The time was six in the evening. It had taken an entire day to work her way through the list. Pulling down the blackout blinds, which Gilbert liked, she closed her eyes.

HOLLY AWOKE TO a rap on the bedroom door. Still in her clothes, she sat bolt upright. Her head ached and her mouth was dry. Quickly opening the blinds, Holly blinked at the daylight outside.

She opened the door and Iris was standing there with a steaming coffee in her hands.

'Hi, Iris.' Holly stared at her. 'What are you doing here?'

Iris looked confused. 'I'm here for work.' She held the mug out to Holly. 'I thought you might like this?'

'Work?' Holly scratched at her tangled mop. 'Thanks, but I mightn't sleep tonight if I have this.' She forced out a laugh. 'No need to check on me by the way. I'm just fine. I'll finish off the rest in a bit. Thanks anyway.'

Iris gave her a strange look. 'Not to worry, dear. I've put all of Michael's roses in vases so that's sorted.' She beamed. 'The house looks great.'

The roses! Holly had forgotten about those. She mumbled something illegible.

'I couldn't find that lovely Waterford vase though. You know the one—it was a wedding present from Gilbert's parents. Have you seen it anywhere?'

There was a small pause. 'I actually thought it would look uh, nice in here. So I, uh, moved it.'

'No problem. I'll bring up some flowers later.'

'No, no,' Holly inspected her thumbnail. 'I'm just... washing it at the moment.'

'Washing it?' Iris looked doubtful. 'I can do that for you.'

'No need. It's just...soaking.'

Iris gave her a searching look before changing the subject. Holly noticed her eyes were a sea-blue colour.

'Would you like me to fix you some breakfast? Perhaps a poached egg and toast?'

Holly gaped. She observed Iris's freshly styled, ash-blonde bob, which was always combed into submission. When she arrived at Larkspur for work each morning it was usually still a little damp from washing.

'A couple of eggs and some toast would be nice,' she replied weakly. 'And a big glass of orange juice would be just the ticket.' She accepted the proffered mug. 'Perhaps some bacon also.' Holly was starving.

'Of course, dear. Would you like it in half an hour or so?' Iris looked fondly at Holly. 'You might like to freshen up first.'

Holly glanced down at the clothes she was still wearing. Sweet, baby Jesus, had she really been asleep since early yesterday evening?

'Sure.' Holly didn't know what else to say.

Iris nodded and retreated. 'Very good,' she said, closing the door behind her.

Holly turned on the shower and tore off her clothes, but not before switching on the television and finding the nearest cable news station to double check the time. *08:56* the ticker said. After a blast of cold water to finish, she dressed and pulled a brush through her hair, wincing as the stiff bristles caught a few tangles. Dabbing on a spot of lip-gloss and a dash of supermarket mascara, Holly considered the things she needed to do that day. There were the application forms for art school, which needed to be filled out. No problem there. She spritzed on some cherry-blossom perfume and sniffed her wrists. Of course she still needed to tie up a few loose ends from yesterday's efforts, too. The deceased Waterford vase under a sideboard downstairs for instance. Holly groaned. She hoped Iris wouldn't spot the shiny heap. The vacuum cleaner was still in her wardrobe and it needed to be put away before Gilbert arrived home tomorrow. Then there were the grubby tea-towels, which probably belonged in the rubbish. Holly would cycle into the nearby village to buy some fresh ones before Iris noticed. The last thing she wanted was for Iris to think she couldn't manage their Wednesday arrangement. As she slipped into a pair of pumps, Holly had a sneaking suspicion that perhaps she had bitten off more than she could chew. Setting her jaw, she headed downstairs.

In the kitchen, Iris was putting away the brush and shovel.

'I found the remains of the Waterford vase,' said Iris. She sounded hurt. 'You should have told me. Accidents happen.'

'I'm sorry,' Holly said after a pause. 'I was going to tell you. I guess I was…embarrassed.' Her face was beet red, and she could feel the fire in her cheeks and all the way down her neck and chest.

'Well, no harm done.' Iris's tone softened. 'You did a great job. The house looks fantastic.' She cleared her throat and rinsed her hands. She began plating up Holly's breakfast.

'Here you go.' She set down the steaming bacon and eggs. 'Orange juice is on its way.' She cut some oranges and put them into the juicer. 'You know, dear, and forgive me if I'm speaking out of turn, but I'm sure you can appreciate what a big job it is keeping this place running smoothly for you and Gilbert.' The machine made its whirring sound as the juice drizzled briskly into the waiting glass. 'And soon you'll be busy with art school and whatnot.'

Holly chewed thoughtfully on her toast. As usual, the food was cooked to perfection although her mouth was a little dry. She wondered where this was leading and gazed uncomfortably at Iris. Her feet twitched.

'I think it's about time we got an extra pair of hands on board to help run the household,' Iris said.

Holly watched intently as Iris carefully placed the freshly squeezed orange juice on the marble-topped breakfast bar. 'Thanks,' she muttered.

'Of course at some point you'll want to start a family and won't be able to chip in every Wednesday anymore. The extra help will be good for everyone.' Iris smiled beguilingly. 'What do you think?'

'Well—' Holly wasn't sure what to say and sensed Iris had the upper hand.

'I could teach you to cook?' Iris offered.

'I can already cook!' Holly sniffed. 'Have you seen these?' She located the biscuit tin and pulled off the lid. 'There.' She planted it on the bench. 'Try one.'

Iris removed a brownie and took a bite. She munched thoughtfully. 'They're really good!' She was surprised.

Holly seized the moment. 'Listen, I know I'm not a house-keeping expert like you. But I want to be involved with running Larkspur. I was raised on a farm and I don't mind getting my hands dirty.' She frowned. 'I don't want to be a trophy on display. I can muck in and help with all sorts of things.' She paused to take a gulp of orange juice. 'I guess you're right though. I underestimated how much there is to keeping this place in order. But I'm a quick learner.' Holly's mother and Gloria had seen to it that she was house-trained. *Time for Housekeeping 101,'* Rosalind would say with a twinkle in her blue eyes, shooing Holly into the kitchen to help Gloria with some baking. Holly had become adept at all kinds of chores, and her mother had insisted Will show her the ropes on the farm, too.

Iris's tone was soothing. 'Come now, no-one's saying you've done anything wrong. I'm just trying to make sure you don't spend all your time getting distracted with housework. Heavens, that's what I'm here for. And before you know it you'll be busy with art school assignments and who knows—maybe even the pitter-patter of little feet?'

It dawned on Holly that she was rocking the boat. Iris felt threatened by her unorthodox interest in housework and in effect, her livelihood. But she was so very bored. Perhaps it was time to take stock of things and find interests that didn't step on anybody's toes or upset the peaceful rhythm of Larkspur.

'Oh, it's too early for that!' she replied. 'But yes, Iris, perhaps we do need another pair of hands around here.' She laughed hollowly. 'Why don't you talk to Gilbert and tell him what you need? I still want the place to myself every Wednesday. But I'll leave the housework to you. I can see I'm not cut out for it.'

Iris looked relieved. 'Of course.'

THAT WEEKEND, GILBERT found the house in perfect order. There were brownies in the tin and blooms everywhere, including in his favourite Waterford vase. Unbeknown to him, Iris and Holly had set aside their differences and searched high and low for a replacement, eventually locating one at an antique shop in Chelsea. Holly had travelled into London to collect the vase, and transported it back to Larkspur with extra care. Knowing how fond Gilbert was of the vase, she wouldn't risk smashing it a second time.

She and Gilbert slept in on Saturday morning, and Holly awoke to the sound of the wardrobe door being opened. She was a light sleeper.

'Morning, sleepyhead.' As always, he was up with the birds. His work had instilled in him an invisible, inner alarm clock. 'What's this doing here?' Gilbert was pointing to the vacuum cleaner nestled inside the wardrobe.

Holly felt a bit like a naughty schoolgirl. Rubbing her eyes she thought fast. 'Oh, that was my fault. I brought it up here when I dropped a...a pot plant.'

Gilbert's brow creased. 'Why didn't you just get Iris to clean it up?'

Holly felt a rush of annoyance. He sounded so very entitled. 'I have two perfectly good hands,' she replied somewhat tersely.

Gilbert smoothed a stray strand of her hair that had fallen over her face. 'My little farm girl.' His tone was amused. 'You know Iris takes care of all that stuff don't you? I don't want you getting distracted from your art studies.'

Holly smiled in spite of herself. 'You're a little prince,' she teased him.

Gilbert kissed her forehead. 'Let's go out for brunch and some shopping.'

'Shopping?' She hadn't been shopping with him before and wondered what it entailed.

A FEW HOURS later, they arrived back at Larkspur with animals in tow. Knowing Holly was not one for material things, Gilbert had steered her towards a pet store, where they bought a pitch-black kitten. Holly named her Middy, short for Midnight, because her eyes reminded Holly of luminous stars in the night sky. In the dark, they were the only things visible on her small furry frame.

On the way home, they dropped by a local farmer's house, who, much to Holly's delight offered her a tiny black Labrador puppy she immediately named Spock on account of his pointy ears. Seeing Holly's pleasure warmed Gilbert's heart, and he was glad he had managed to snatch a few moments to arrange this little sortie from his hotel room in Tokyo earlier in the week. He had been spending rather a lot of time there lately. For some reason, the locals seemed to like him and his boss was pleased with the work he was doing there.

Chapter Four.

JUST SIX MONTHS after their wedding Holly awoke feeling nauseous. Feeling both excited and terrified she phoned Tammy, who advised her to take a pregnancy test. So it was that a queasy Holly drove to the local pharmacy to buy a pregnancy test kit. Back at home she peed on the plastic stick. Two pink lines appeared momentarily, indicating she was in the motherly way. She phoned Gilbert's office, but was told he was out to lunch with clients. She then called her parents and Rosalind answered with a crisp hello.

'Hi, Mum! Guess what?'

'Hello, darling. Good to hear from you. What's up?'

'I think I'm pregnant!'

Rosalind almost dropped the receiver. After a pause she said, 'Congratulations, darling! She couldn't help asking, 'Was it planned?' Rosalind was pleased at the prospect of becoming a grandmother, but also a little concerned that her barely 20-year-old daughter was growing up so quickly and was no longer their little girl.

'It wasn't planned, Mum, but it doesn't matter.' With nervous excitement, Holly continued. 'It's all so strange!' She paused. 'Did you feel that way when you were expecting?'

'Of course, I was slightly older than you when you arrived so I suppose I had a bit more time to get used to everything.'

There was a small silence before Rosalind changed the subject. 'Does Gilbert know?'

'I called his office, but he's with clients.'

Rosalind sensibly steered the conversation away from Gilbert and offered plenty of sagely advice, including tips on how to beat morning sickness and what foods to avoid.

After speaking with her mother, Holly decided to take a nap; she would tell Gilbert the news tomorrow. She left a message with his personal assistant for him to call back the next day. Late the following morning the phone rang.

'Gilbert, we're going to be parents!'

The news took a second to sink in. As soon as it did, Gilbert was thrilled.

'That's brilliant!' he exclaimed. 'Are you feeling okay?'

They discussed their news excitedly.

'I'll be home early on Friday night,' he promised before saying goodbye.

Gilbert immediately told his personal assistant to hold all calls for an hour. With typical efficiency he personally set about locating the best midwife money could buy. He held off on finding an interior designer for the minute. When the baby's gender was known, one of the spare bedrooms would be turned into a nursery—ideally a blue-coloured one.

That weekend the couple happily debated whether to hire an interior designer, or if Holly should decorate the nursery herself. Holly won. With her artistic flair it was only fitting that she should do it.

After twenty weeks and many more mornings of nausea later, Gilbert and Holly learned they were expecting a girl. Holly was thrilled. However, to her surprise, Gilbert seemed a little subdued.

'What's wrong?' she asked, puzzled.

'Well, I was just hoping, first child and all, that we would have a boy.' He wanted an heir. 'We can always try again after this,' he said.

'Not so soon.' She glared at him. 'I've only just got my head around the fact I'm twenty and already expecting my first baby.'

Gilbert realised at once that he had made a mistake and backed down. 'Of course, of course.' He hugged Holly apologetically. 'Forgive me for being selfish.'

Good-naturedly, Holly forgave him. She usually looked for the best in others, and expected the same in return. So far she had managed to bounce back from all of life's knocks, not that she had encountered many during her sheltered life. Sometimes she forgot how lucky she was.

THAT FRIDAY NIGHT Gilbert downed a single-malt whiskey in his wood-panelled study. He removed his tie and navy-blue jacket, which were custom-made by a tailor in London, who also picked out his ties, shirts and socks. He poured another drink from a fine cut-crystal decanter. He had decided to hold off breaking the news to Holly. The promotion at work meant he would be required to travel even more frequently, often outside the country, to manage some of the bank's most valuable clients. The step-up was a major one for Gilbert, one that even his pregnant wife could not deter him from.

As Gilbert saw it, everyone had a certain checklist of dreams that they wanted to fulfil. For many, those dreams would remain elusive. For some, the disappointment came early in life. For others, it came quite late. Some couldn't bear the thought of failure and so never really tried. Gilbert never quite understood that mentality. He reckoned inertia was the archenemy of dreams. Others tried and failed and yet still managed to acquire new dreams along the way. It was the lucky ones who were the winners, the kinds of people who triumphed over obstacles and whom others admired. Gilbert saw himself as a lucky one.

His mind drifted back to the cold, creaky corridors of his childhood home. He shuddered. Yes, he adored Holly and she would always have the best that money could buy. As for the new addition to the family, well, that was unplanned but not a problem, he thought, pouring himself another whiskey. Providing financially for his family was the most important thing in the world to Gilbert. It would not do for Holly to work for a living unless she really wanted to. And, in a few years' time, he would be able to buy his parents' estate twice over. Although he had no intention of going near that falling-down pile unless absolutely necessary, the mere satisfaction of knowing he could was enough.

The following morning he broke the news of his promotion to Holly.

'We need to talk,' he said firmly. Holly knew that the serious expression on his face foreshadowed the nature of the conversation that was to follow. The morning seemed to grow a shade greyer and a slight frown darkened Holly's expression. She had inherited the trait from her father, and it annoyed her that it betrayed her inner-most feelings.

'About what?' she enquired, gulping a mouthful of decaffeinated coffee. Looking suspiciously at Gilbert, she drew the soft white duvet to her chin and made an effort not to frown.

Taking a deep breath, a determined look settled on Gilbert's handsome features. His mouth tightened at the corners and a small furrow appeared on his brow. He met Holly's gaze. 'Would you like the good or bad news first?'

'Good news, please.'

Gilbert touched her hand.

'I've been promoted, Holly, something I've been wanting for ages. It's a bigger salary, and it means you won't have to work if you don't want to, and I'll arrange a generous allowance for you to do with as you please.' He smiled hopefully at her and tried to suppress the tense look on his face.

Holly immediately guessed where the conversation was headed. Her frown deepened.

'An allowance?' she croaked. 'And, the bad news?'

'The promotion becomes effective after the baby is born,' Gilbert began. It was against his better judgment to postpone, but in his clinical banker's mind it was a show of good faith and commitment to Holly.

'And what does your promotion entail, exactly?'

42

He explained it meant more travel and time abroad.

Holly erupted.

'Now it seems you'll spend even less time with me! With the baby!' She began to cry, and Gilbert tried to comfort her. She pushed him away.

'Why can't you wait until the baby is at least six months old before you totally desert me for your job? I hardly see you already!' Her voice was filled with anger.

Gilbert's mouth was a tight line. He had not for a minute expected this conversation with his pregnant wife was going to be easy.

'Look, I'm sorry you feel this way, but if I don't grab this promotion I could end up in the same position for years. Just think, it will provide us with greater financial stability, incredible holidays together, and we'll never want for anything. I could even look forward to an early retirement and more time with you and the kids.'

He stopped and focused on her.

'You do want another one, don't you?'

'Not if I am going to raise our children on my own.'

With that, Holly extricated herself from their breakfast in bed and stalked from the room, slamming the door so hard that a picture slid off the wall. Gilbert winced. He had always been uncomfortable with theatrical displays of emotion.

JUST A FEW days later, Gilbert kissed his wife goodbye and departed for yet another overseas business trip. Holly waved as Gilbert's new silver Mercedes crunched down the gravel driveway and disappeared from sight.

Loneliness washed over her like a tidal wave. This was not how marriage was supposed to be, she thought. Stroking her baby bump, Holly contemplated calling her parents, but decided against it. After all, she was supposed to be a grown woman who could cope on her own.

Holly trudged inside and went to Gilbert's study. Normally this room was Gilbert's domain and she left him to it, but right now she wanted his things around her. Spock joined her there. She slumped into Gilbert's big leather armchair, disrupting Middy, who meowed indignantly and leapt to the floor. Spock sat beside the chair and gazed up at Holly with sympathetic brown dog-eyes. Holly sat despondently for a while, trying to make sense of everything. Once in a while Spock licked her hand. Eventually, she moved stiffly from the armchair, tripping over Middy, who darted out the door.

From an enormous bookshelf, Holly plucked a novel Tammy had loaned her some time ago, which had somehow found its way into Gilbert's study. Reading aimlessly, Holly soon realised it was in fact a saucy tale about a woman having a clandestine affair with a handsome older man. Pausing, a terrible thought came to her. Was Gilbert having an affair? Surely he must be lonely with all that time abroad?

'Stop it!' she told herself sternly.

HOLLY MOPED ABOUT the house as the days dragged steadily on. Constant morning sickness depleted her vitality and appetite. She felt increasingly isolated and began sleeping for longer and longer stretches at a time. When Rosalind realised what was happening—thanks to a discreet phone call from Iris—she rushed to Larkspur. She was alarmed by Holly's depressed condition, and inwardly fumed at Gilbert. How could he desert her daughter when she needed him most? She knew Holly was sensitive, but had never before seen her daughter quite so down. With her practical, school-teacher ways Rosalind determinedly set about jollying Holly from her melancholy. She decided to install a routine, one that gave Holly things to look forward to. Having company and conversation at mealtimes was as good a place as any to start.

Holly's baby bump grew as the colourful nursery took shape under her creative hands. Rosalind and Iris observed Holly tackle the project with increasing enthusiasm.

'Gilbert should be told,' Rosalind remarked to Iris.

'Probably best it comes from you,' Iris replied.

Rosalind nodded judiciously. 'Yes, you're probably quite right,' she agreed. 'Probably quite right.'

LABOUR CAME SUDDENLY one evening. Fortunately Gilbert was home at the time. His sister Fiona was also staying at Larkspur—she had just returned from Dubai and was between contracts with high-profile accountancy firms. Holly and Gilbert had agreed to have her to stay while her London apartment was being rented out. After all, they had no shortage of space for guests.

Lucy Bette Tatton was born in late October. From the outset she was a happy baby with bright blue eyes and wisps of blonde hair. Once Holly returned home from the private hospital, visitors began dropping by and everybody wanted a turn holding the child. Lucy was content to lie placidly in their arms, smiling, dribbling and waving her chubby little limbs in the air. Proud grandparents doted on her, and even the normally aloof Tattons were enthralled. Surprisingly, Mrs Tatton thawed out and with every visit she bestowed indulgent smiles and nonsensical baby talk upon little Lucy. When it happened, Gilbert and Holly's eyes met in private moments of mirth. It was a wondrous, sleep-deprived time and they were completely and utterly besotted with their tiny bundle of joy. Gilbert was glad he had postponed his promotion and wangled two weeks off work to spend time with Lucy and Holly, or 'his girls' as he called them. For once, work could wait.

AS HOLLY BREASTFED Lucy in the large and leafy conservatory she contemplated her sister in law. Fiona was staying on at Larkspur while Gilbert was away in Tokyo finishing off some business deal there. She had hoped to strike up a friendship with Fiona, but was forced to conclude that was unlikely. Holly soon discovered Fiona was dispassionate about almost everything that interested her. Try as she might, she couldn't break through to Fiona who, while polite to the point of perfection, was not really an affable kind of person. A few shared words over a cup of tea every now and then would have been pleasingly sufficient. However, Fiona was up without fail at the crack of dawn every day for a workout. And yet, her apparent remoteness could be beguiling. Beneath her uptight demeanour, she watched everything and was a keen observer of facial expressions and body language. She listened to other people's conversations and every now and then offered helpful advice. Sometimes people were a bit surprised when she spoke. Occasionally she even attempted to tell a carefully constructed joke, but unfortunately there was no sense of timing or emphasis, and her punch lines frequently fell flat. She was also obsessed with food and thought it fascinating to discuss what she ate for breakfast, lunch and dinner. When the subject arose, Holly's eyes glazed over and she escaped to change Lucy's nappy or feed her in the privacy of the nursery.

Lucy smiled broadly during a break in breastfeeding, as if she understood her mother's unspoken confession. Lucy didn't care so long as mother's milk and an endless shower of little kisses kept coming. As far as she was concerned, Mum was perfect.

'WHAT A DAY,' Gilbert thought as he loosened his tie in the privacy of his six-star hotel suite at the Mandarin Oriental in Tokyo. It had been filled with business meetings and client entertainment. He was also a touch jetlagged, but a good night's sleep would soon fix that. Tomorrow Gilbert and his clients would be driven deep into the Japanese countryside for some traditional massage and relaxation at a boutique spa. He was looking forward to that. Work was increasingly demanding since the promotion and he found it all too easy to forget about his personal life.

Gilbert found business trips to Japan to be the most challenging. There was a veritable minefield of rituals and etiquette that had to be followed, lest somebody be offended. Fortunately Gilbert had done his homework, as it were, on how the Japanese conducted business. He quite liked the business card routine, which involved holding out your card with both hands and offering a small bow when giving it. When receiving a business card, you studied it fully to show respect.

In Japan, he found it was important to enquire after your client's family before getting down to business. He made mental notes on his clients' families, their daughters and sons, and was always able to personalise such conversations, which meant he was held in high regard. Much of his business was done at the dinner table, but he never tried to close a deal over a meal. Privately, Gilbert felt Japanese business lunches were unnecessarily long, and he was quietly amused by western businessmen who unwittingly breached one of the many protocols.

Earlier that day he found himself enjoying a long lunch with a pair of Japanese businessmen.

'My wife, she love sashimi,' commented Yako, one of his clients. He was beaming with enjoyment, and a tiny drop of soy sauce had found its way to his fleshy chin.

Kinto, the other, nodded vigorously.

'Mine too. Only her favourite is teppanyaki; she eat it whenever we go out.'

'What your wife's name?' Yako enquired. 'She like sashimi?'

Gilbert paused before replying. 'She likes all Japanese food very much.' It was true; Holly adored going to sushi restaurants—in fact when they were courting they had been to a lot. They hadn't been since.

Yako and Kinto nodded approvingly.

'She has good taste,' Kinto said.

'Do you have picture of her?' Yako asked.

Gilbert guiltily realised he had left it back at the hotel

47

room. It was his favourite picture of Holly, the one he had taken during their Maldives honeymoon.

'It's in my hotel room,' he said.

The men looked disappointed. Yako removed a gleaming wallet from his vest pocket and slid a small photograph from it.

'Hana,' he stated, holding out the picture to Gilbert. A surprisingly young and serious face with long straight black hair looked back.

'Very beautiful,' Gilbert said.

Kinto, too, held out a photograph of his wife for Gilbert to inspect. An older, but nevertheless attractive face stared from the card.

'Also very beautiful.'

'Getting old now, but still good woman,' Kinto replied, looking pleased. 'Do you have children?'

'Yes, a daughter,' he replied. 'Tomorrow I will bring photos and show them to you at lunch.' He knew full well that he was due for another long lunch session.

The conversation made Gilbert feel unexpectedly sad, as if he was missing out on something important. Here were Kinto and Yako smiling, slightly drunk and both pleased to be going home to their wives later that evening. When they turned out the lights before sleep, their wives would be lying beside them, breathing and warm. At that moment Gilbert really missed Holly.

AFTER A GLASS of water and a gulp of fresh air for tea Fiona removed her thick layer of makeup. What she did next was neurotic. Her marauding fingers crept rakishly across her face, transfixed with the delicious opportunity to plunder pimples, real or imagined. This procedure could last for up to an hour at a time. When finished, Fiona's face was blotchy and red. She tore herself from the mirror. The damage was enormous. Because of the often-daily sessions, her skin was terrible. It had to be caked with makeup to conceal the blotchiness, which aggravated things even further. Fiona consequently harboured feelings of self-loathing and disgust, interlaced with an ever-present urge to continue this pimple-popping habit.

Stepping back from the mirror, she inspected her wounded face and winced slightly.

'Thank God for foundation, and at least I'm thin.' She whispered to herself.

She critically inspected her skinny, underwear-clad body from every angle. Her mind wandered back to when she was growing up. Back then, her body was plump and metal braces occupied her teeth. She squeezed out a smile at the thought of her improved self. There was still work to do, however. More workouts for starters. She wondered if Holly might like some helpful tips on how to regain her pre-baby body and resolved to ask her in the morning.

AFTER LUCY WAS tucked up in her cot, Holly checked her emails in the downstairs study. Usually there was a message from Gilbert every day. Holly was counting down the days to his return in a week's time, and then seven days later he would be jetting off again, this time to Stockholm. She was annoyed by Fiona's skulking. In fact she could hear Fiona creeping around in her en-suite bathroom upstairs. Holly was curious to know what kept her there for such long stretches of time, particularly in the evenings. Wriggling the computer mouse, the screen flared to life. She noticed Fiona's email account was open. In the Sent Items folder her eyes fell on a message that Fiona had sent to Gilbert.

The subject line was curious: *Update*. Glancing around, Holly contemplated what to do next. Should she read it? Fiona was a woman of few words and Holly sometimes wondered what she was thinking. Curiosity got the better of her and Holly guiltily clicked the email open.

Dear Gilbert,

Holly is perfectly well enough for me to leave Larkspur in two weeks' time. I've been offered another contract in Dubai and I'm keen to take it. You should be reassured that Holly is no danger to herself or to Lucy. It seems she has a supportive mother, who visits frequently. I am also sure Holly will be delighted to see you in a week. She speaks of you often. I hope you don't mind me saying this but I'd like to remind you that not everyone is as strong as you or I. Everyone is different.

Fiona x

Holly was stunned. Was this the reason Fiona was at Larkspur? To spy on her? Holly dropped the mouse and bolted from the study to the lounge and sat there on a plush sofa in the darkness. Her mind was working overtime, and then she spotted Fiona's rakish frame creeping down the stairs, no doubt to log out of her email account. Sure enough, Holly heard the study door open and then, minutes later, close again.

Stifling the urge to scream, Holly scurried outside where she almost expected the night to appear as ugly as she felt inside right then. Instead a silvery moon shone high in the vast indigo sky, which was dotted with stars, as if some great unseen hand had scattered them there. Wind gusted through huddled trees, which sounded like they were whispering secrets to one another. Crisp air was spiced with the aroma of leaves, woods and earth. The night's beauty was completely lost on Holly, who lashed through grass blades and across fields.

A lone fox watched from a safe distance, its eyes like glowing orbs in the moonlight. Her ancestors had lived long on the land, and survived numerous brushes with hunting parties. The wary fox soon turned and trotted into the darkness.

Holly stopped, sufficiently far from the house that she could only see its lights as specks in the distance. She screamed. It was a release, of sorts. Taking several deep breaths, she screamed again. This time it was in frustration at Gilbert's prolonged absences from Larkspur and his underestimation of her as a capable person who had thoughts and feelings and dreams all of her own.

She decided then that she would no longer be grateful for the little scraps of Gilbert's time and attention that fell from his work desk. She knew she was entitled to more, and have it, she would.

Chapter Five.

ROSALIND FOX WOKE feeling unwell. She wondered if it was part of 'the change.' She had been unusually tired and out of sorts over the past few weeks. Shoving her glasses on, Rosalind inspected herself in the dresser mirror. Her stomach was unusually puffy and tender to touch.

When Gloria arrived for work that morning, Rosalind shared her concerns as she struggled to eat a soft-boiled egg and toast.

'Gloria, I'm a bit unwell,' she said with a yawn. 'I've booked a doctor's appointment this afternoon at four o'clock—do you think you could drive me there?'

'Of course. Is everything alright?'

Rosalind paused. 'Just a bit out of sorts.'

Gloria looked concerned. 'Well dear, it's no problem at all for me to take you to the doctor this afternoon. Would you like to lie down in the meantime? I can bring you in a spot of lunch later on if you like?' To her surprise, Rosalind accepted and Gloria pottered about the big old farmhouse while Rosalind rested.

ROSALIND ENTERED THE doctor's office with a sense of foreboding. She told him the problem and he enquired about her general health. Then he asked her to lie down while he examined her tummy.

'Mrs Fox, I can't say definitively what the problem is, but we'll need to get some blood tests done right away.' He scrawled something on a form. 'Please give this to the receptionist and tell her to pass it on to the nurse, who will see you next.'

Rosalind handed the form to the receptionist, who in a well-practiced motherly voice asked her to be seated for a couple of moments while she arranged for a blood test.

Gloria sought to reassure Rosalind when the women were driving home afterwards.

'It's probably just the change,' she said, steering the car.

'Well, I certainly hope so,' Rosalind said.

Both women were inwardly anxious. However, each held the view that there was no point making a fuss until the test results were back. Until then, things would go on as normal.

Sure enough, the evening continued as any other, with Gloria and Rosalind making lamb cutlets and roast vegetables together. Rosalind ate what she could, which was very little indeed. Nevertheless, she seemed to perk up a little. Gloria usually left for the day once dinner was prepared, but today she stayed on for the meal. She spent three days a week working at the Fox's and appreciated their company and her modest earnings. She enjoyed her duties and their companionship. She was a homely soul with a pleasant face and faded blue eyes. She liked looking after people and in her spare time was involved in her local community, where she helped with the church flowers and organised events such as harvest. After the meal, Gloria helped with the dishes, said her goodbyes and then trotted stoutly to her car in the cool evening air.

THE DOCTOR'S SURGERY phoned for Rosalind. They asked her to return as soon as possible to talk through the test results. That afternoon Rosalind drove herself there. She was an immensely practical woman; no point worrying about something until there was ground to do so.

She reported to reception and moments later the doctor summoned her to his office, where she sat down. Gently shutting the door he proceeded to tell Rosalind in kind but factual terms that the test results strongly suggested cancer. More tests were needed to be certain of the diagnosis.

For a second, Rosalind thought he was joking.

'I beg your pardon? Cancer?' Her bright blue eyes squinted with disbelief.

The doctor was ill at ease. He coughed softly into his hand.

'It looks that way, Mrs Fox. I am sorry.'

'Can it be treated?'

'We're certainly going to do our best, but we need to arrange further tests right away. Can you come back tomorrow?'

Rosalind knew that she had to tell her husband and family. The prospect was daunting; she didn't like fuss.

'And if the tests confirm your suspicions?'

The doctor cleared his throat and studied his hands uncomfortably. 'Then you will need treatment.'

There was a long pause.

'Might I—might I die?'

'Mrs Fox, please take a few deep breaths. I realise this is a terrible shock. Take a moment to digest this.'

Rosalind looked directly at the doctor.

'Might I die?' she repeated.

'I'm afraid it's always a possibility, Mrs Fox. Tomorrow's tests will give us more clarity, so until then it's best to remain calm.'

It seemed a futile thing to say, and Rosalind tried to remain calm. It was not easy. She felt breathless.

'Th—thank you, doctor. That—that's difficult news. Very difficult indeed.'

'I understand it's no simple matter.' The doctor looked genuinely sad. 'Mrs Fox, here are some information booklets. There will also be professional support available should you and your family need to talk to anyone. And, if there is anything else you need, please let me know right away.'

He stopped and waited half-expectantly for a reply that didn't come. He saw Rosalind was gripping the chair.

'Do you need someone to drive you home?'

Rosalind considered this. 'Perhaps that's a good idea. I feel...rather rattled.'

'Of course, I'm not surprised at all. Would you like to use the phone?'

With a trembling hand, Rosalind dialled her home telephone number, which was answered quickly.

'Gloria, it's Rosalind. I'm at the doctor's. Could you come and get me?'

If Gloria thought Rosalind was acting strangely, she hid it well. 'Yes, of course, dear. I'll be there right away.'

Twenty minutes later Gloria appeared. They made small talk during the brief ride home. Upon arrival, Gloria busied herself with brewing a pot of strong tea while Rosalind sat silently at the kitchen table. Cups, saucers, utensils, milk and sugar were deftly laid out on a pressed floral tablecloth. A steaming pot of tea was produced.

Sitting with Rosalind, Gloria waited patiently for it to stew. Momentarily, she poured two cups and placed one in front of Rosalind, who absentmindedly added a little milk. She stared at her cup.

'Gloria, it's horrible. Just awful.'

'What is it, dear?'

A muscle twitched in Rosalind's cheek. 'I have cancer.'

Before Gloria could reply, Will appeared at the door, stomping the mud off his Wellingtons. Leaving them outside, he stepped into the kitchen wearing his favourite old socks. He didn't immediately notice the two women's sombre mood. When he removed his hat, his shock of silvery hair looked to be in need of a good combing. He smiled when he saw them there.

'Is there enough tea for an old man like me?'

Windswept days were regular in the Surrey countryside and they made him feel particularly alive.

'Of course, Will,' Gloria said. 'Take a seat and I'll just

get you a cup and saucer. There's plenty to go around.' Placing the utensils in front of the now-seated Will, she poured his tea and waited for him to take a sip.

'Biscuit?'

'That would be lovely.'

Gloria made sympathetic eye contact with Rosalind, unsure of what to say next. The biscuits rattled on the bone china plate. Will took two, and extended one of them to his wife.

'Rosalind, would you like one?'

'No, thank you.' She looked forlorn.

Gloria cleared her throat.

'I'm afraid Rosalind isn't feeling well.'

Will looked concerned and fixed his gaze determinedly upon his wife. 'What is it, dear?'

Tears welled in Rosalind's eyes. She wished it were all a bad dream. But, it wasn't the case and there was no escaping. She exhaled and prepared to break the most difficult news of her life to her husband.

'Will,' she said gently. 'I have something to tell you.'

Without being asked, Gloria discreetly left the room.

'Is everything alright?'

'No…' Rosalind began to weep softly. 'I have cancer.'

Will frowned and scratched the back of his neck while he digested the terrible news.

'What? When did you find out?' His good mood had vanished completely, replaced by fear and anxiety.

THE NEXT DAY, Will escorted his wife to the out-patient's clinic for an endoscopy. When the test results were returned, they revealed advanced cancer. It had taken seed in her stomach, and spread to other organs. The specialists at the hospital reasoned that she probably had a three percent chance of survival.

Back at home, Will comforted his wife in silence, with his arm around her shoulders and a grim expression on his face.

'Holly and Lucy are coming over this Sunday,' he said heavily. 'I suppose we'll have to tell them.'

'I can't bear it,' Rosalind said. Normally she looked forward to Holly and Lucy's visits; this time she was dreading it.

Will was devastated. That evening he went outside to check that the hens were in their pen for the night. He took far longer than normal to do so. The prospect of a future with no Rosalind, his wife of nearly thirty years, was hopeless, terrifying, glum and altogether too much to bear thinking about. He closed the gate firmly and trudged back up the path and towards the old farmhouse.

LATE ON SUNDAY afternoon Holly and Lucy arrived with overnight luggage. Apprehensive about breaking the news, Rosalind simply couldn't pretend all was well. She glanced around the warm kitchen. She and Will had lived here for decades and had raised a daughter. Happy memories were everywhere.

She welcomed Lucy and Holly inside with her usual hugs. They sat at the worn oak kitchen table and Lucy began playing with the dried flowers that had not long been strung from the ceiling. Gloria wasn't working that day, so Will brewed the tea.

Holly immediately sensed something was amiss.

'Is everything okay, Mum?'

Revealing her illness was the moment Rosalind had been dreading for days. She had gone to great lengths to conceal her dark under-eye circles, however she couldn't disguise her puffy and papery skin no matter how much blush she applied.

Glancing out the window, she observed an airplane steadily soaring across the fading blue sky, a diamond in the last rays of sunlight.

'I'm afraid not. I really don't know how to tell you this but I'll do my best, so please bear with me. I have cancer of the stomach—and—and there's a three percent chance of survival.'

Rosalind looked away, pained. Will squeezed her arm, trying to offer comfort.

Holly felt a hollow disbelief. Instinctively, she moved to hug her mother. Lucy followed suit.

Rosalind was determined to not cry. Holly was sobbing softly. Lucy remained silent, but for a small crease on her brow. They silently embraced, while Will watched.

Presently, they released one another and wiped damp eyes.

'Tea?' Will asked.

'Hot chocolate, please,' Lucy piped up. She had special frothy hot chocolate made by Granddad, exactly how she liked it. Will poured the drinks while Rosalind explained what had transpired over the past two weeks. Holly sipped her tea and did her best to remain calm.

WHEN BEING TUCKED into bed later that evening, Lucy had only one question.

'Mummy, Grandma is going to die like Baxter, my goldfish, isn't she?'

Holly avoided using the word 'die' whenever possible. But the facts were obvious to all, including the ever-curious Lucy. For a moment Holly considered whether she should spare her daughter the horrid details and pretend that Grandma was going away for an endless summer vacation of sorts. In the end, she decided Lucy deserved diplomacy. Some years earlier, Lucy had learned about death when she had discovered Baxter floating in his bowl one morning. Holly had had to explain that Baxter wasn't coming back, ever. They could get a replacement fish, she'd said, but good old Baxter had swum off to other shores.

Finally, after all questions were answered and careful explanations given, Holly kissed Lucy goodnight and stumbled off to bed. She lay under the covers for a while, staring at nothing in particular. She tried to read a book, but struggled to make sense of the increasingly blurry words on the pages, and gave up.

She recalled asking her mother delicately how long she had to live. Rosalind vaguely replied that it depended on how well she responded to treatment. Perhaps another eighteen months, she had suggested. Eventually Holly fell asleep. She dreamed in grey and black.

ROSALIND'S TIREDNESS INCREASED as the days passed her by, one after the other, at an all-too-steady clip. Some days she lay in bed until Will came in from the farm or the tool shed, usually wearing his favourite brown gilet. Gloria found endless reasons to poke her head through the door, to ask questions she already knew the answers to, to chat about topics of varying importance and to inform her whenever she left the house. Rosalind could see the concern in her eyes.

Rosalind grew to appreciate the frequent interruptions; it was hard not to let her mind wander to all sorts of places, some happy and some oppressive. 'Why me?' she wondered in between.

There were many days when she thought of her long-gone youth as she rested. She recalled events she hadn't thought of in years. When she was a little girl, her school class went on a farm picnic. They'd planted their small bottoms amongst cowpats and ate egg sandwiches, followed by delicious little jellies in a cup. There had even been cold sausage rolls, which she recalled had pleased her taste buds a great deal. She remembered how all the food in her lunch bag had smelled of the crisp, ripe apple packed next to it. It had been a hot summer's day and the bees zipped from clover flower to clover flower. Some of the children had tried to catch them. One of the boys was successful and got stung. What a commotion! His hand had puffed up and turned as pink as the clover flowers. Thereafter, everyone was a bit more careful, and had left the bees to their chores.

Holly visited as often as she could. She didn't live too far from her parents, about an hour by car and the same by train, once you accounted for all the fiddly stops and station changes. But that didn't mean she could accept what was happening.

It occurred to her that her mother was spending a lot of time in bed when one day Rosalind described in detail the dynamics of a large family of sparrows she had been observing closely, which were living in the hedge outside her bedroom window. Holly thought about this. Coping meant carrying on normally when in fact she was constantly stressed. Her father was the same. They were not a family who freely expressed their feelings.

Sometimes Holly even managed to convince herself that her mother would be around for a long time yet. She cooked nourishing casseroles and stored them in little containers in the freezer as snacks for Rosalind. The freezer was full of them, and there was always freshly cooked food in the kitchen, given by well-intentioned friends and neighbours who hoped to fatten Rosalind up. Rosalind had lost a lot of weight. She was very thin and needed morphine for the pain.

Holly gazed silently at all the containers stacked inside the freezer.

'She doesn't eat them,' Gloria said, stating the obvious.

GILBERT CONVINCED HOLLY to take a short holiday, which was designed as a distraction of sorts. They escaped the rainy English springtime and flew to Morocco for a three-day break. It was a new experience for both of them.

At the village market, Holly was awed by the numerous brightly-coloured fabrics on display in the ramshackle stalls. Cunning merchants immediately pegged her as a soft-touch foreigner. They mobbed her, trying to place their wares in her hands as if to convey some sense of ownership and close a sale. Somehow she ended up holding a small Arabic lamp made from low-grade brass, and attempted to hand it back to the seller.

He refused it. 'You like, you buy.'

Holly sighed. 'How much?'

He told her. The price was high, but she wasn't comfortable with haggling, and paid.

The merchant wrapped the lamp in crinkled tissue paper and handed it to her with a toothy grin.

'Maybe there is a genie,' he said.

Other merchants looked on enviously, and clamouring voices and grasping hands soon surrounded her. She briskly walked off in the general direction of the hotel, forcing herself not to respond to any more sales pitches.

'My sandalwood is best in the market!'

'My spices are guaranteed make you stronger!'

'Try my snacks, you will not regret it!'

Back in the hotel, Holly told Gilbert of her adventure. He was slightly amused. She showed him the lamp and wryly explained a genie was supposed to appear when the lamp was rubbed. She wished it were true.

WHEN THEY RETURNED home, Holly was shocked by her mother's condition. She almost cried when she saw Rosalind so frail and her once lustrous, black hair so lank and thin. In actual fact her mother's condition hadn't worsened in the three days Holly was away. It was just that Holly's holiday had worked a little too well and—however briefly—she had forgotten her troubles. Gloria's hours had been increased, which meant Rosalind could remain at home in comfortable surroundings that were familiar to her. Holly now understood the end was near; how could she not have seen this more clearly? She put on a brave face and greeted her mum with a hug.

'Sit with me, Holly. Tell me about your holiday.'

Holly gave the lamp to her mother and told her about the persistent street vendors in Morocco.

'Lovely, lovely.' Rosalind smiled and shifted her head on the pillow. 'I'm glad you and Gilbert were able to have some time together. I've always thought that the day-today life could wear you down. You need to keep making an effort not to take each other for granted.'

She then changed tack completely.

'I think a lot about when I was a little girl. All sorts of memories I thought I'd forgotten have come back to me.'

'Like what?'

'You know, things have changed so much these days. Everyone just wants to be entertained. In my day we had to entertain ourselves.'

Sixty-three days later, Rosalind died in her sleep. Will woke at dawn, switched on the bedside lamp and looked over to his wife. She was still, eyes closed, and with a peaceful expression.

'Oh Rosalind—'

Tears slipped down his weather-beaten cheeks.

'Rosalind—'

With the tips of his fingers he carefully brushed aside what was left of her hair, and lightly kissed her forehead. The Rosalind he had loved so much, and for so long, was gone. He would never see her shining blue eyes again.

'Goodbye, my darling, I will miss you...'

Chapter Six.

IT WAS MANY months before things settled down after Rosalind's death. Holly sobbed on and off while Will was quietly consumed by his thoughts out in the paddocks. Even Gloria wasn't her usual bustling self. She missed Rosalind dearly, but worried more about Will and Holly. It was best to keep busy, she thought, and with that set about her daily duties. As for Will, acquiring Sarge was the turning point in him coming to terms with his grief. With Gloria's quiet support, he slowly found a renewed interest in life and began fixing those niggling household tasks she couldn't attend to herself. He and Holly even made a pact to quit smoking.

Lucy usually stayed with Will whenever Holly was painting night and day to prepare for her art exhibitions— she had long since finished art school. Gloria often ended up looking after Lucy while Will was off on the farm attending to his chores. As for Holly, painting was a kind of therapy; it gave her a sense of expression and empowerment. If life didn't make sense, at least her art did and it was something she could control.

After her training, Holly began to carve out a small niche for herself in the art world. Acrylic and oil paints were her favourite mediums. She was particularly adept at capturing people in unguarded moments, such as train commuters reading, sleeping, listening to music and looking tired after a long day's work.

Somehow it struck a chord with critics as being 'insightful and zeitgeist.'

Gradually her work became sought after by a small but growing number of collectors who appreciated her talent. In time, Holly began to receive a trickle of invitations to exhibit her work at prestigious London galleries. She accepted and worked furiously to complete her collections. She had long since installed a small art studio at Larkspur. With a sort of rebellion, she had had the carpet ripped from a surplus downstairs room with French doors opening out to a walled garden. It gave Holly a certain satisfying sense of contentment to be utterly immersed in her work. On weekends and after school, Lucy would sit and adoringly watch her mother paint. Holly kept a small painting of Lucy on her studio wall. She had painted it one sunny afternoon during school holidays when the pair were picnicking in a hay field. Lucy was laughing and her blue eyes contrasted vividly with the golden grass.

A painting of Gilbert also hung on the wall. Holly had persuaded him to sit for her one rare weekend he was home. He was reading a chunky weekend paper on the deck, and the light caught his blue-green eyes and captured his handsome, unreadable expression. Most weekdays Gilbert would stay at an apartment he had bought on London's Southbank, overlooking the River Thames. It made getting to and from work easier because he typically worked twelve to fourteen-hour days. When he wasn't away on overseas business trips, he drove home to Larkspur on weekends, to spend time with 'his girls.'

It dawned on Holly that she and Gilbert had grown apart. She could see it in his eyes, which turned a mossy-green colour whenever they made love. When he gazed at her, it sometimes felt as if he were a million miles away. She understood his mind was probably on work and wished for the umpteenth time he was in the moment with her. Needless to say, Holly had decided long ago to get on with her life without complaint.

'No-one likes a nag,' she reasoned. Only occasionally did they argue.

ABOUT A YEAR before Lucy's accident, Holly travelled to London. It was the night of their sixth wedding anniversary and Gilbert had managed to finish work early. Lucy was staying with Will for the weekend.

Dinner was booked at a nearby restaurant overlooking the river. The evening was clear and crisp, and city lights blazed against the darkening sky. Holly was dressed for the occasion in a shimmery pink dress and shiny tan ballet pumps. Her hair fell in natural waves and she looked healthy with little make-up and just a dash of scent. She had long since ditched her supermarket mascara and assortment of perfumes. Nowadays she wore a more grown up rose fragrance. Gilbert gazed at her appreciatively as she was seated.

The waiter took their orders and they chatted for a few minutes until their drinks arrived. Gilbert fiddled with his silver cufflinks and Holly wondered if he was listening to what she was saying about her current art exhibition and Lucy's latest school achievements. A faraway expression arranged itself on Gilbert's handsome features, and Holly resisted the urge to shake him back to the present. Then the food arrived and she began taking deliberate mouthfuls. Suddenly she was seized with a sense of panic. Who was this man she had married? She was no longer so sure.

'Don't you ever wonder what it must be like to be more than just an occasional weekend family man?' she blurted.

Gilbert paused from his salad, and placed his fork on the starchy white tablecloth. He met her eyes.

'Holly,' he warned. 'We're covering old ground. Do you really want to go there again?'

'Sorry,' she mumbled. 'I don't know what came over me.' She tried to think of something else to talk about. 'Did you know I've been invited to exhibit my work at the Soleste Gallery?'

He played along. 'No, I didn't. That's wonderful! When did this happen?'

'Two days ago.'

'Why didn't you tell me?' He sipped at his red wine and eyed her over the rim.

'You were at work.'

Gilbert put the glass down and gazed intently at her. He opened his mouth as if to say something, but Holly beat him to it.

'It's not as if you're really part of my life anymore, Gilbert.' That hurt, she could tell. But she didn't know whether it was her words, or the public setting.

'Do you mind? We're supposed to be out for our anniversary meal and you're spoiling it by starting a fight.'

'Sorry,' she mumbled again, looking guiltily at her butternut risotto.

The conversation was strained during the remainder of dinner. Gilbert paid the bill, and they strolled in silence alongside the riverbank towards his apartment.

Holly had visited it only twice since he had bought it. She observed how sparse and devoid of clutter it was. Clearly he had made some effort for her because there were fresh flowers and expensive scented candles in every room, some still in their wrappers. Gilbert's usual navy suits and crisp white shirts hung in the main wardrobe. She removed her shoes and sank into the leather sofa. Gilbert lit some candles and filled two flutes with champagne. He handed one to her. She took a gulp and braced herself.

'Gilbert,' she said. 'We need to talk.'

'It's not the same old stuff again is it?' He groaned.

'I need to tell you what's on my mind, Gilbert.'

He was silent for a moment. The candles glowed beguilingly. Grudgingly he agreed. 'Go on, then,' he said, his emphasis on the last word.

'How much longer will we do this for? Living separate lives, I mean. I don't struggle for anything, and everything is taken care of. Lucy goes to the best school, my art career is going well and I have a lot to be thankful for.' She could tell Gilbert was getting impatient, but continued anyway.

'There's something I want that money can't buy. It's you, Gilbert. You. How much longer will we go on living separate lives? I've been patient, faithful and just carried on with my life as best as I can without you. But I miss you, Gilbert, I really miss you.' She began to cry.

Gilbert looked aghast. Once again he struggled to understand his wife. She had everything she wanted, did she not? If he really wanted to, he could retire in the next three years and they could continue their comfortable lifestyle. He decided to tell her that.

'Holly, don't cry.' He put his arms around her. 'Perhaps I could retire from my job in a few years and do something else, closer to home.'

She stopped crying and looked at him with hope and trust in her eyes.

He melted. 'I miss you too, Holly. I wish I could spend more time with you and Lucy. If I could change that I would, but it's my job.' He hugged her soothingly.

Holly nodded and tried to understand. She liked being listened to by Gilbert. He brushed away her tears with his thumbs. Gently he kissed her eyelids and then her lips. It had been a while for both of them, and soon their clothes were on the floor.

HOLLY HAD MADE several acquaintances through art circles. One of them was connected to a well-known journalist named Lewis Wagnall, who wrote for a popular women's glossy magazine. Through a mutual acquaintance in art circles, Lewis asked if he could write a feature article about the personality behind the canvas.

Holly was an intensely private person who selected her friends carefully. She was all-too self-conscious about her unusual arrangement with Gilbert and didn't want anyone prying. Other than close family, the only person aware of Holly's personal life was Tammy, who by now was a successful London advertising executive. They usually caught up whenever Holly travelled to London for her art exhibitions. It was Tammy who finally convinced Holly to do the interview, saying it would help raise her profile as an artist.

A TRENDY BLUE sports car zipped up the driveway and swung into spot just inches short of one of Michael's carefully pruned hedges. The driver's door swung open and a man in his late-twenties leapt out, looking roguishly dishevelled. He surveyed the scene with a measured eye, taking in the imposing house, gardens, glasshouses and outbuildings.

The front door at Larkspur opened and Iris appeared. She waited for the visitor to approach. When he did, he held out his hand. The other grasped a leather satchel.

'Pleased to meet you. I'm Lewis Wagnall.'

'And I'm Iris. You're here to see Mrs Tatton.' She gave a small sniff.

'Yes I am.' He shook Iris's hand with practiced charm. He was handsome in a slightly clammy way, with a smile that didn't quite involve his eyes.

'Come in,' Iris said, a little on the defensive.

She led him to the spacious conservatory, where Holly had arranged for the interview to take place. Iris left him waiting and went and busied herself with making tea.

After a few moments Holly breezed into the leafy room. Not long showered, she looked fresh and natural.

'This is one of my favourite rooms,' she declared, extending her hand with a smile. 'Holly.'

'I'm Lewis. Pleased to meet you, Holly.' He looked around. 'Nice conservatory.' He shook her hand before sitting down, his eyes darting over her face and body. She wore leggings and one of Gilbert's old shirts, which was nipped in at the waist by a belt. Her still-damp hair was in a messy knot, and her feet were clad in battered leather boat shoes. Holly looked every inch the artist.

Iris entered the room with a steaming pot of tea and cups on a wooden tray. She set it down on the table and left wearing a mildly disapproving expression. She didn't really trust journalists, their silky way with words and their meanings.

THE INTERVIEW STARTED, tentatively at first and Lewis gave a disarming opening gambit. 'Tell me about your increasing recognition in the art world,' he said.

Holly began to describe how once she finished art school she had thrown herself into painting. Before long she had enough work for an exhibition, and she contacted a few galleries with details and photographs of her work. Three said no, but the fourth, an up-and-coming gallery in Brixton, agreed to a meeting. A day or two after seeing her work, they had agreed to an exhibition. Three quarters of Holly's collection sold quickly, and an art dealer from another London gallery, this time in Marylebone, invited her to do a follow-up exhibition. She had just three months to put together a new collection, during which time Iris helped Lucy with her homework and ran her to and from ballet classes. Weekends and term breaks for Lucy were often spent at the farm with Granddad, and she liked his company.

Lewis appraised his subject with pale, merciless eyes.

'Tell me about your daughter. Is she an inspiration to your work?'

'Yes, certainly.'

'Your husband? I believe he is an investment banker in the City. I take it he is proud of you?'

Holly frowned, feeling a little unsettled. She didn't quite know how to answer his question, and tried not to give her apprehension away. Studying her small, paint-stained hands, she began to say something. Lewis pounced on her indecision.

'I understand you have a unique arrangement with him, whereby he lives in London during the week and travels a lot for business. Does this have an influence on your work?'

From out of nowhere, Iris appeared with a plate of walnut bread and laid it politely on the table, her eyes blazing protectively in Lewis's direction.

'Freshly baked,' she said coldly.

He returned Iris's barely veiled hostility with a practiced smile. He had been in this situation a thousand times before.

'Thanks, Iris,' Holly said gratefully.

Iris lingered for as long as possible before leaving the room.

Holly reached for a slice. With easy, coiled movements Lewis did, too. His fingers brushed against hers. His gaze quickly raked her body once more, taking in her slim neck and petite waist, before meeting her eye. She quickly withdrew her hand. He settled back into his seat and smiled reassuringly. He was enjoying Holly's obvious unease.

'Where were we? Ah, that's it. You were telling me about your husband.'

Holly guardedly explained that Gilbert was very supportive and emphasised how lucky she was to have the freedom to pursue her dreams. Lewis listened intently.

'Does he come to your exhibitions?'

'He's very busy.'

The subject was closed and Lewis sensed the finality of her tone. Nonetheless, he decided to press further. 'Has he been to one of your exhibitions?'

Now that he mentioned it, Holly realised Gilbert hadn't attended a single exhibition. Not even the first.

'Sometimes,' she fibbed.

'Which one was that?'

'It was about a year ago. Look, can we move on? I don't see how this is relevant, and I told you, my husband is a busy man.'

The interview went on for a further forty minutes, during which time Lewis took some shots of Holly in her studio. Lewis's pale, all-seeing eyes roved the room, taking in the portraits of Lucy and Gilbert on the wall by her easel. The only thing missing was a portrait of the family together. He made a mental note of this.

He took a photo of the paintings.

'Please don't,' Holly said. 'They're personal.'

THREE WEEKS LATER, the article ran. The headline read *Poor Little Rich Girl and Artist.* Cold horror crawled through Holly's body as she continued reading. Lewis had obviously done his homework. He had somehow discovered various 'sources close to the family,' who were obviously willing to gossip about her. The piece focused less on her artistic achievements and more on her private life. It discussed her marriage and the fact she and Lucy were on their own most of the time. It mentioned that Holly was the much-younger wife of a wealthy, well-connected city banker and implied his moneyed and powerful connections had helped her career. There was even a photograph of her painting of Gilbert. It had been cropped to look like a police mug shot.

Holly's face burned red with humiliation and anger. She slammed the magazine into the bin. How did this happen? She racked her brains. Was it something she said? Did she give off the wrong impression? She thought she had been so careful with the information she disclosed. Instead the story had been twisted, sensationalised. She vowed to distance herself from all media in future.

When Iris saw the interview she was furious and told Michael as much over morning tea.

'I told you journalists weren't to be trusted.'

Michael chimed in, 'Why don't you suggest Holly gets an agent to screen her from all of this nonsense?'

'Why yes, that's a very good idea.'

HOLLY'S MOBILE PHONE trilled. It was Tammy.

'I'm so sorry I talked you into it Holly. I swear I want to club that smug weasel Lewis over the head with a dictionary and stick pens in both his eyes.'

'You're not to blame, Tammy. I'm just dreading Gilbert seeing the article.'

At that moment the landline rang. 'I have to go.'

It was Gilbert's mother. 'I read the article about you.' The voice on the end of the receiver quivered. 'It's not quite what I expected.'

Holly sighed. 'It's not quite what I expected either, Mrs Tatton.' She tried to explain what had happened.

'I didn't realise Gilbert was away so often.'

For the first time it occurred to Holly that Mrs Tatton might feel excluded from their lives. Gilbert was obviously distanced from his parents, too. When it came to birthdays and Christmas, Holly dutifully took care of cards and gifts. She found herself apologising for not being in touch sooner and promised to visit that weekend.

With a heavy heart she then phoned Gilbert to tell him about the article before he found out by some other means. His voicemail was on. Holly left a message.

Later that evening he phoned back.

'I read the article.' His voice was cold.

Holly's heart sank. 'I didn't mean for it to happen.'

'It's downright embarrassing. I cannot believe my own wife would expose our personal, private life for the world to see.' He was fuming.

Holly felt sick. She tried to explain it wasn't the story she expected; the reporter had sold it to her as a friendly interview, and she was told beforehand it would focus on her artistic accomplishments.

'I'm getting an agent to screen any press interviews from now on,' she added, hoping it would ease matters somewhat.

'In my position I simply cannot afford to have negative publicity. It could be damaging to my reputation. I want a retraction printed.'

Suddenly Holly was furious. 'It may not be what you or I wanted, but getting a retraction will be damn near impossible!'

'My lawyers will contact the magazine.' His tone was ominously calm.

'Will you tell them what was printed is actually untrue?'

There was a tiny pause before he replied, 'I will make sure this goes away.'

'And how do you imagine I feel about all this? Do you think I wanted this to happen?'

He ignored her again. 'I'll call you back tomorrow.'

Sure enough, he did, first thing, and got straight to the point.

'This Saturday morning, the editor of that cheap rag will interview us together. This time the story will focus on our achievements as a couple.'

'But I promised we'd visit your parents!'

'Cancel it. It's arranged. See you then.'

Holly frowned at the receiver as she hung up.

THE REPLACEMENT ARTICLE ran three weeks later. The phone calls started up again, but this time it was people saying what a 'lovely article' it was, how talented they were and how wonderful she and Gilbert looked together.

Mrs Tatton seemed placated when they visited her and Mr Tatton in their ramshackle old country home in the middle of nowhere. As their car approached the house, Lucy asked her parents if it might fall down one day. Although she didn't say much or smile often, it was clear old Mrs Tatton was pleased to see them. It occurred to Holly that she might even be lonely. Mr Tatton's hearing had deteriorated quite badly, but he refused to wear a hearing aid. Everyone had to shout and poor Mrs Tatton had to repeat nearly everything that was said in a loud voice so he could hear.

'No need to shout,' he grumbled a few times as they ate Beef Wellington with silver cutlery in the draughty, oak-panelled dining room. Its faded grandeur was rather depressing.

It was a far cry from Holly's childhood, which was filled with fun, play and laughter. She had grown up with the warm glow of her parents love and approval. Now, for the first time, she had an inkling of what lay behind Gilbert's no nonsense character.

Chapter Seven.

HOLLY GRABBED HER car keys from beside the front door. She made her way to the garage where her Audi TT was parked. Holly loved to drive and her car afforded her a degree of freedom that London's often over-crowded public transport system didn't.

Zooming along the M2 towards Lucy's hospital was an almost enjoyable experience until she hit the busy, narrow streets of inner city London. Holly silently prayed that Lucy would be conscious when she got there.

Arriving at the hospital and swinging nimbly into an available car park, she scraped through her purse for loose change to pay for parking. A small pile of pennies glinted coldly from the bottom of her purse.

'Great!' Holly exclaimed under her breath when she found a stray £50 note in the glove box.

Unfortunately, the parking machine didn't provide change for overpayment. She would have to dash to a nearby store and break the note into smaller change. Glancing around, Holly spied a cluster of shops and made her way toward the nearest one. Dr Robert emerged from the doorway of a sandwich bar. He stopped when he saw her.

'Back again?' His smile was professionally friendly.

'Hello, Dr Roberts.' She returned his smile. 'Afraid so—how is Lucy?'

'Ah yes, she's stable, which is good. We're keeping a close eye on her, don't you worry.'

'Thank you.' Holly was grateful for his care and hesitated before asking tentatively, 'Is there any improvement?'

'It's probably a bit early to say, Mrs Tatton. But we're looking after her.'

'You can call me Holly.'

'Holly. And how are you?' He smiled reassuringly.

Dr Roberts knew from experience that changing the subject was a useful distraction for him and the anxious family members of his patients.

'I'm…fine,' she ventured, a little too brightly. Then her face fell. 'Well, actually, I'm really worried about my daughter.'

'Which is natural, don't worry. She'll be okay.' Glancing at his wristwatch, he said, 'I'm heading back to the ward now actually. Do you remember the way?'

Holly thought she did, but decided to walk with Dr Roberts anyway. His presence was reassuring. 'I need to pay for parking,' she said.

Dr Roberts observed the £50 note in her hand.

'Good luck breaking that around here.' He smiled wryly. 'Do you have something smaller?'

Holly shook her head. Rummaging in his pockets, Dr Roberts extracted some shiny pound coins.

'Change from my lunch. If it helps, you can borrow it.'

Feeling slightly embarrassed, Holly reluctantly accepted the money and thanked the doctor. Touching her lightly on the back, he escorted her in the direction of the parking machine, and then the hospital. He walked with her until they reached the entrance of Lucy's ward.

'You really didn't have to.'

'Don't mention it.' For the second time, Holly noticed his kindly grey eyes.

'Push the buzzer if you need anything. Bye now.'

Holly watched as he strode down the polished linoleum corridor. Before turning the corner he glanced back and smiled briefly. Embarrassed to find she was still staring

Holly scurried into the ward where Lucy lay sleeping, surrounded by machines and tubes. For hours, Holly remained at her daughter's side. Chapters from her favourite book were read, songs were hummed. She even massaged Lucy's small feet. Eventually, Holly exhaustedly dropped her forehead on the sheets, wishing she could crawl onto the bed and nap alongside her daughter.

'You heard the doctor.' Her dad's gruff and familiar voice roused her. 'No point trying to wake Lucy quite yet.'

Holly leapt to her feet. 'Dad!' she exclaimed. Hugging her father, she then looked at him intently. 'How did you get here today?'

Will was once more in possession of his Volvo, and today he had journeyed to the hospital in a more civilised fashion. Sarge was tied up outside the main entrance and under the watchful eye of the hospital security guard. Will had learned his name: Brantley. Brantley liked animals and he approved of Sarge. He didn't mind keeping an eye on the dog whenever its owner was inside.

'Dad, do you mind if I go outside for a cigarette?'

Will gave her a funny look, and nodded.

The glass doors at the hospital's main entrance slid open. Holly stepped into the sunlight, which weakly attempted to shine from behind a cloud. Lighting a cigarette and glancing at her cell phone, she realised there was no reception, which would explain why she had heard nothing from Gilbert all day. Wiggling her phone in one hand she dragged on her cigarette with the other. Still there was no reception. In the end she tried turning the phone off and then on again to restore the signal.

'The signal's not very good around here,' Brantley volunteered helpfully. 'But you might get one over there, by the seats.'

Holly thanked him and noticed Sarge nearby. Giving him a pat, the little brown and white dog wagged his tail vigorously and licked her hand, which tasted of cigarettes.

Holly's cell phone trilled. It was Gilbert.

'Where have you been?' He sounded frantic.

'I'm so sorry, Gilbert. There's no reception at all inside the hospital, which is why you haven't been able to reach me. I've just managed to get a signal now.'

'It's okay,' he said. 'I was concerned about your whereabouts, that's all. I wasn't sure where you were.'

'I'm fine. Where are you?'

'Just leaving Heathrow and I'm on my way to the hospital. How's Lucy?'

Holly explained everything. She sensed Gilbert's worry and sought to reassure him, focusing more on the positives and rather less on negatives.

Gilbert absorbed the information and then asked, 'Do you think Lucy will be alright?' He liked facts.

Holly considered what to say next. 'Dr Roberts says she seems stable and the best thing we can do right now is try not to worry.'

Of course she knew it was easier said than done.

WILL WAS OUTSIDE checking on Sarge when Gilbert arrived, and Will showed him to the ward. Holly and Gilbert embraced when they saw each other.

'How's she doing?' Gilbert asked.

'Sleeping…I mean…in a coma.'

'I know.' Gilbert's tone was soothing. He smiled distractedly at the ever-present nurse at Lucy's bedside. 'Where's the doctor?'

Holly explained that in about ten minutes time Dr Roberts would probably pass by on his regular patient rounds and that Gilbert would be able to speak with him then. Together they sat at Lucy's bedside. As it turned out, Gilbert had managed to get five days special leave from work.

'Shall we stay at the Southbank apartment this week?' Gilbert looked hopeful. 'It will make visiting Lucy much easier if we stayed together.'

Holly protested she didn't have any spare clothes or toiletries with her. She also liked the comfort of Larkspur.

The empty London pad just reminded her of their separate lives.

Gilbert waved his hand. 'Just buy a few things.'

Despite his best efforts to persuade her, Holly insisted that she return to Larkspur for the night to pack an overnight bag and feed the pets.

'I'll come with you then,' Gilbert said. He ran a hand over his brow.

Holly saw the exhaustion in his eyes. 'No, you should get a good night's sleep here. I'll stay over with you tomorrow.'

Eventually she kissed Gilbert and her father goodbye, and made the long drive home. She had been at the hospital since early that morning and would be back again first thing the following day.

'I had hoped Holly would stay with me at the apartment,' Gilbert remarked to Will.

'Aye. Well, in case you hadn't noticed, she's become quite independent these days,' Will replied drily. He liked it that his daughter was standing on her own two feet. It was one less thing for him to have to worry about.

SURE ENOUGH, HOLLY appeared at the hospital early the next morning. Dr Roberts was checking on Lucy when she arrived.

'Morning, Dr Roberts.' Holly greeted him, trying to sound chirpy.

'Bright and early again, I see.' His tone was friendly. 'Hopefully you had enough spare change for parking?'

Holly smiled. 'I'm organised today.' She tried to repay him the coins he had given her yesterday.

He shook his head.

'They fall out of my pocket all the time.' Changing the subject, he enquired, 'Have you come a long way?'

'From Guilford, but I'll stay in London the rest of the week.' She gestured to her overnight bag. 'My husband has an apartment on the Southbank.'

'Gilbert? Ah yes, we met yesterday afternoon and I explained the details of Lucy's condition.'

'How is she today?' Holly's heart pounded somewhat erratically and she rubbed her chest lightly.

'Still waiting for the swelling to go down some more, but everything seems to be going in the right direction.' His tone was reassuring. 'Sometimes they remember the coma as if it was a dream, so it helps to have you here.'

Smoothing his unruly blonde hair, he quietly noted the tell-tale signs of fatigue on Holly's face. Although she had carefully applied makeup, it was difficult to disguise the dark circles beneath her eyes.

'And how are you this morning?' he asked.

Holly gripped her handbag tightly and took a couple of deep breaths.

'Fine, busy. I'm supposed to be preparing for an exhibition at the moment, but that's not going to happen.' She made a face and fiddled with her necklace.

Dr Roberts observed her small, paint-stained hands. 'You're a painter?' he enquired curiously.

She examined her fingernails. 'How did you guess? They're impossible to clean.'

Dr Roberts smiled at Holly and then cleared his throat. 'Well, I'll carry on—remember to use the buzzer if you need anything.'

HOLLY GLANCED AT her wristwatch. Where was Gilbert? It was late morning and she had expected him at the hospital some time earlier. Remembering there was no cell phone signal, she made her way outdoors to call him. Gilbert answered the phone, groggily.

'Where are you?' Holly asked.

Gilbert apologetically explained that he had overslept, having gone at least twenty four hours without rest as he had hurried home.

'It's okay,' Holly said. 'I have my overnight bag.'

'Great. I'll call you when I'm on my way. Need coffee.'

Hanging up, she remembered once more that there was no phone signal inside the hospital. She texted Gilbert:

Take your time, Lucy is doing okay. See you later.

GILBERT RESTED HIS head on the soft pillow and read the message. Work had been taking its toll on him of late; city bankers were not seen as the pioneers of prosperity anymore. Before the downturn they were sought after, admired and celebrated. Women chased them, men aspired to their status, and politicians and the media alike pandered to them. Before the crash, bankers were synonymous with hard work and hard play, and a lifestyle of free-flowing money. The party was in full swing back then, Gilbert remembered. Now, he was just plain tired.

Towards the end of the boom years, the level of excess had blown out of control. Banks lent money for anything and to almost anyone. Frenzied house buying ensued, prices soared and the bubble ballooned. Of course it was inconceivable that such heady extravagances should continue indefinitely, but nobody seemed to be too bothered by that.

The market collapse was as brutal as it was swift. All of a sudden everyone was trying to hop off the merry-go-round of free credit and easy cash. Now, the once-glamorous title of investment banker held little allure, and politicians and the media rounded savagely on the banks and bankers and their excesses.

As he lay in bed, Gilbert, exhausted as he was, considered himself lucky to have kept his job when many of his colleagues hadn't. He also counted himself lucky to have kept his wife. Some wives had married their husband's wallets and once the money ran out, so did their wives. Fortunately, the company he worked for had resisted the temptation to overload their books with risky investments, which meant it could manage its exposure to toxic assets. Even still, hundreds of millions of pounds had been wiped from the company's books.

Gilbert, however, had done well from the recession, even if his bonuses were clipped. He had bought Larkspur long before the housing bubble took hold, which meant he hadn't paid too much and wasn't financially overextended when it burst. His private investments were an essay in care and in foresight and continued to grow in value even in the darkest days of the recession. In fact, he saw the recession as an opportunity to make even more money from his careful private investments.

By contrast, Holly was not all that interested in money. Whenever Gilbert shared news of a successful investment, she would roll her eyes with boredom. Theirs was a traditional marriage in that Gilbert handled the couple's finances, while Holly raised their daughter and, with Iris's assistance, ran Larkspur. He liked it that way; Holly was a good woman and he was pleased with his choice in a wife. But every now and then he had the feeling that things were not quite as they should be.

Staring at the apartment ceiling and trying to motivate himself to get out of bed, Gilbert remembered Holly as the young, impressionable woman he had married all those years ago. He liked to imagine her in that pink dress, with flowers in her hair. But times had moved on, and they had gradually drifted apart. All of a sudden, tired or not, he knew he had to see her, talk with her, listen to her. He also wanted to see Lucy, to see her golden hair and hear her carefree laugher once more.

Chapter Eight.

THE SMALL WHITE car rattled and revved for miles up the M1. Sniffing the air, Sarge recognised petrol, fear and musty car smells. He could smell something else among the rubbish on the floor. What was it? Hamburgers, that was it. He knew the aroma; it reminded him of his owner, Will. Sometimes he too had hamburgers and left the wrappers in the car for days. Sarge buried his nose in the waxy paper and inhaled deeply. The smell was familiar, but where was Will? Instead he was in a strange vehicle with a lanky man. He knew the man's scent; he had sniffed him a few times outside the hospital. It was a friendly smell—not very familiar though. The man and Will sometimes talked to each other.

'Good boy,' the man would say occasionally, patting him on the head. Sarge sometimes wondered if all dogs were named 'Good Boy.' It was then Sarge scented his hands. Sweaty—a different sweat than Will's—earthy, musky, and with a hospital high note.

Something wasn't right. The man behind the wheel was driving erratically. Sometimes he would moan, 'Me mam, me poor mam, no, no, no, no.' Tears would course down his treacle-coloured cheeks and he would thump the steering wheel with his palms.

No, this was not normal behaviour, observed Sarge. Nonetheless, he sensed he wasn't a bad man because Will seemed to like him and he had a certain meaty smell about him. People who didn't like dogs emitted a certain, sharp smell—rather like vegetables on the turn. Sarge didn't particularly like vegetables, although he was partial indeed to the roast potatoes Gloria sneaked him when she thought Will wasn't looking. Unbeknown to her, whenever Gloria wasn't looking, Will would also slip leftover roast potatoes to Sarge. Sarge was extremely grateful either way. He would wag his tail discreetly, lick his chops and gaze appreciatively at the bestower of such tasty treats. Of course, the roast potatoes were gone in seconds, gulped down with barely a chew.

'How on earth do you taste anything?' Gloria would say, patting him affectionately.

Right now, Sarge knew that Will and Gloria were a long way away. He didn't understand why he was in this strange man's car. Somehow he sensed he wasn't supposed to be there either. Feeling unsure, Sarge let out a whine, pawed the backseat debris and then uneasily settled on the grubby seat. Ordinarily he rode in the front, sometimes even on Will's knee when no-one was looking. He knew his owner would be missing him right now. Sarge whined again. The man heard him and stopped moaning.

'You hungry?' he asked.

Aware the man was talking to him, but unsure of what was being said, Sarge rested his head on his paws. He looked up with hopeful brown eyes and feebly thumped his tail on the backseat.

A few miles later, the small car swerved into a fast food outlet. Sarge sniffed the air, which was wonderfully meat-scented. Momentarily, an aromatic and juicy hamburger was dumped on the back seat in front of him. Not quite believing his luck, he quickly glanced around and then gobbled all of it, not caring that it was probably too hot for his pace. The man looked on approvingly.

'Good boy,' he said and patted him.

Sarge knew those words. He panted and wagged his tail. The hamburger made him feel better.

HOURS LATER, THE overworked and overheated vehicle rattled to a halt outside a narrow terraced house, which was painted a dull crumbly yellow. The man huffed momentarily in his seat. Sarge watched with puzzlement as he blew his nose, threw tissues on the floor and then combed the short, springy layer of hair covering his scalp.

Sarge observed a beefy woman, wearing large, purple earrings, emerge from the house and waddle towards the car. She had big, springy hair and it framed her skull like a dark globe. She tapped on the driver's window.

'Brantley, my boy!' her big voice commanded. 'Step on out here!'

Opening the door and extracting himself from behind the wheel, Brantley threw himself at the rotund women and tightly embraced her.

'Hello, Aunty Tilda.' They stayed like this for a moment and gently swayed in the cool night air while she patted him on the back and made soothing noises.

Then, disentangling herself, the woman curiously eyed Sarge who was sitting in the untidy backseat.

'Who's that?' Peering through the backseat window, her breath fogged the glass. Sarge cautiously thumped his tail on the layer of rubbish.

Brantley studied his feet and tried to remember the dog's name. He knew it started with an 'S' and said the first thing that came into his head.

'Uh, that's Steve.'

Aunty Tilda looked at Sarge who wagged his tail hopefully. He yearned to get out of the car and obligingly she opened the door. Without delay, he leapt to the ground and urinated on one of the car tyres. Brantley immediately grabbed his collar. A gentle breeze carried the scent of the woman, who smelled meaty and of something else he couldn't quite place. In fact, it made him feel a little uneasy. His tail stilled.

'Is he is your animal?'

Brantley looked everywhere but at Aunty Tilda. Sarge surreptitiously licked a smear of hamburger juice off the top of one of his shoes.

'Nah,' he said. 'On loan. A friend said I could have him for a few days.'

The woman pressed her lips together and narrowed her eyes. She smoothed her large black and orange tunic, and gazed intently at Brantley, who tentatively looked back at her. Eventually she patted Sarge on the head.

'Good boy.' Sarge's tail wagged back and forth. She smelled of all different kinds of spicy and unfamiliar food. 'Good Steve.'

Inside the crumbly yellow house, a dozen or so people were gathered. Somehow, they had managed to squeeze into the small front room, on sofas, spare chairs and beanbags. A large silver-framed picture of Brantley's mother was propped up on a gleaming cabinet. She was a sombre looking woman, not unlike Brantley, with wide, dark eyes and a pointed chin. Several candles surrounded her image and reflected in the glass, giving it an eerie glow.

Brantley stood still for a moment while the people took turns embracing him and murmured comforting things into his shoulder. He was very tall, taller than everyone else in the room in fact. Sarge was very small in comparison. Sarge hesitated, unsure whether to sit down or go off and explore the many and strange new room smells.

The rest of the evening was uneventful. Sarge, or rather 'Steve' as everyone now called him, was later fed some spicy chicken stew in the kitchen by Aunty Tilda.

'You didn't bring any doggy food for the animal?' she asked Brantley, scooping chicken leftovers into a plastic bowl on the floor.

'I forgot,' he replied weakly.

Aunty Tilda wagged a finger at him. 'Your mother would have a fit, you bringing this animal here unannounced, no proper food or anything. Lord, he might have fleas!' She looked genuinely horrified at the prospect.

At the mention, Sarge obligingly scratched his neck. Like most dogs worth their salt, he definitely had a flea or two. It came with the territory.

'He's sleeping outside!' Aunty Tilda shrieked.

Brantley's hand stiffened on Sarge's collar. 'He can't do that. He has to sleep inside,' he protested. 'With me.'

Aunty Tilda gave the same look she had given him earlier, pressing her lips together and narrowing her eyes. Intently observing Brantley's pinched face, she relented. It was tough enough losing a niece, let alone your mam.

'Alright then, but tonight only.'

Later, Aunty Tilda wondered aloud, 'Who calls their pet Steve? That's a man's name!' She shook her head. 'And what kind of person just gives away their pet to somebody for few days? Seems mighty strange to me.' She muttered these things to the soap suds in the kitchen sink after everyone had gone home for the night.

NEXT MORNING, SARGE woke and gnawed his hind leg, which felt somewhat itchy. The carpet in Aunty Tilda's spare room was the scratchy kind, unlike the softer stuff he normally slept on at the foot of his master's bed.

Reflecting on Will made Sarge feel sad and lonely. Here he was, with a new name, in a strange city, and with strange people, who were kind enough.

The room gently reeked—last night's hamburger and spicy chicken stew hadn't been kind to his normally sturdy, canine stomach. Brantley opened the window and flopped on the bed. Sarge whined and gazed with anticipation towards the mound of blankets covering Brantley. He wasn't sure what he was expecting; just any kind of action would do, preferably of the walk or dog-food variety. Instead, he heard some kind of snuffling. Brantley was sobbing into his pillow. Sarge recognized the same words he had repeated last night.

'Me mam, me poor mam, no, no, no, no.'

Many dogs have the built-in ability to sense human distress. Sarge was one of those types. Brantley's large hand protruded from the blanket and Sarge padded over to it. He nudged it with his nose. The moaning stopped. Brantley's bleary-eyed face emerged from the tangled mess of sheets and blankets, which had twisted and turned in the night.

Sarge sat for a long time as Brantley's hand stroked his furry neck and caressed his soft ears. The weeping eventually subsided. At this point, Brantley hauled his lanky frame from the bed, scratched his backside and stumbled from the room.

Meanwhile, Aunty Tilda was greeting the day's mourners as they trickled through the front door. Last night she had prepared an enormous tray of jerk chicken, ready for tomorrow's oven and the many hungry bellies she had yet to cater for. Sarge sniffed the air. His tail drooped ever so slightly when he detected the aroma of spicy smells. The bedroom door was slightly ajar and he could hear the sound of water running in the other room. Taking his chances, Sarge slipped through the door and crept stealthily down the stairs, his eyes darting about. He froze when a shadow darkened the doorway.

'Not so fast, pooch!' said the shadow in a stern voice. Distracted by thoughts of escape, Sarge weakly wagged his tail to indicate he was friendly. Aunty Tilda huffed towards him and caught his collar. Her hand brushed the metal disk attached to it.

'What's this now?' she muttered to herself. The disk was small and shaped like a bone. Examining it closely, a hissing noise escaped her lips, which smelled of the fried plantains she ate for breakfast. She read out loud the words, which were engraved on the small metal bone:

MY NAME IS SARGE
If found call number overleaf

'Brantley Green!' she bellowed at the top of her lungs.

One of the mourners in the other room poked her head around the corner. 'Everything alright, Tilda love?'

The bathroom door opened a crack. Brantley's fuzzy head poked through.

'Everything alright, Aunty Tilda?' he asked.

Politely dismissing the curious mourner with a nod and a wave, Aunty Tilda decided it would be best to discuss this matter out of earshot.

Huffing and puffing, she hauled her body up the stairs. By now, the bathroom door was wide open. Brantley stood in his boxer shorts and t-shirt, with the shower running behind him. Sensing trouble brewing, Sarge hung back meekly behind Aunty Tilda's well-rounded legs, encased in black leggings.

'Turn off that damned shower, Brantley Green.'

Not used to hearing such language from Aunty Tilda's normally exemplary lips, he hurriedly obliged.

'We need to talk. You want to do it here or in private?'

Wisely choosing the latter, he obediently trotted to his bedroom and flopped on the bed.

Aunty Tilda lowered her generous rump on a chair in the corner. It was draped with Brantley's clothing, by now badly creased. Sarge panted at her wide, slipper-clad feet.

She said one word, 'Sarge.'

When Brantley heard he paled and swore.

On cue, Sarge stood, looked at her expectantly and wagged his tail vigorously. He was back! Did this mean Steve was no more and he was Sarge again and he could go home to Will? Excitement got the better of him and he let out a short, sharp yelp. Rather embarrassed at the high-pitched sound, he looked the other way and hoped that nobody noticed.

'Don't you go using cuss words now, Brantley.' Grasping Sarge's collar she said quietly, 'Did you bother reading this before you took him?' She gestured to the engraved metal disk.

Brantley's pointy chin quivered. 'I didn't mean to take him, honest Aunty. I wasn't thinking when I got the phone call; I just grabbed the dog and ran.'

'Ran from where?'

Brantley looked sullen. 'Hospital.'

Aunty Tilda gasped, 'Your JOB?'

Sarge's excitement abated when he realised a conversation between two humans was taking place and he wasn't part of it. He sighed and settled at Aunty Tilda's large, slippered feet.

Brantley closed his eyes. Tears escaped from the corners of his eyelids and trickled down his unshaven cheeks. They splashed on his t-shirt.

'I made a mistake,' he said in a small voice. 'I'm sorry.'

Unsure whether to whack him over the head with one of her purple velveteen slippers, or comfort the poor boy, sympathy won out and Aunty Tilda hugged her grieving nephew. Brantley sobbed into her pudgy shoulder.

Again Sarge heard the words, 'Me mam, me poor mam, no, no, no, no.' Benevolently he licked Brantley's hand, which dangled by his knee.

'There now,' Aunty Tilda said consolingly. She stroked his springy black hair.

'You'd best call the number on the collar. That dog has a rightful owner, and he's probably real worried about his whereabouts.'

Brantley looked terrified.

'Brantley Green,' she insisted. 'That animal has an owner wondering about his whereabouts.' Aunty Tilda looked stern. 'And you have responsibilities. Re-spon-si-bil-i-ties. Your job—if you still have it that is. You'd better 'fess up before it's too late. In fact, you should be calling right now and doing it.'

Her words had the desired effect. Brantley sat up a little straighter. He rubbed his eyes with his wrists.

Aunty Tilda studied his terrified face and pulled out the big guns. 'What would your mam say? She didn't raise no criminal boy now, did she?'

Brantley froze. Knowing he was cornered and some-thing had to be done to rectify the mess he had gotten himself into wasn't pleasant. If he didn't toe the line, Aunty Tilda would tell Uncle John who would tell cousin

Tandi, who would then tell the entire family. Then everyone would know he had stolen someone's pet and he would never live it down. They would whisper and gossip and say things like, 'That was a nice dog you bought with you to Leeds when your mam passed on. Whose animal did you say he was again?' He shuddered at the thought.

'I can't,' he whispered. His tone was pleading. 'I mean, I want to, but I can't telephone those people right now. Can't I just call them tomorrow?'

Aunty Tilda shook her head in firm disagreement.

Brantley sighed. Never before had he felt so vulnerable in all of his twenty-something years. An idea popped into his mind. 'Could you do it? You've got a way with words, Aunty Tilda.' He spread his palms imploringly. 'Please don't make me do this today.' A lone tear rolled miserably down his cheek.

Aunty Tilda was about to say, 'Brantley Green, get on that telephone NOW.' But she stopped before the words came out of her mouth.

Instead she said, 'Brantley Green, someone's got to make some phone calls ASAP.' She shifted in her seat. 'The longer you leave it the more trouble you'll be in, see.'

Brantley nodded and opened his mouth to speak, but Aunty Tilda cut in.

'So,' she commanded. 'I will call the number on Sarge's collar and you will give me your boss's number.' She waggled an outstretched hand expectantly. 'Now please.'

'Thank you, Aunty Tilda,' he whispered piteously.

'Don't you ever try this again.' Her tone was ominous. 'You get it together now. I know losing your mam is tougher than tough. But I'm grieving too because I lost my niece and you don't see me going AWOL now, do you?'

Brantley shook his head agreement. 'No, ma'am.'

'The world doesn't revolve round you. Being sad doesn't give you the right to go doing dumb things.'

'I'm sorry.' He studied his toes, thoroughly chastened.

'Just be glad I haven't told Uncle John. Now give me your boss's number and get in the shower and clean yourself up. We have guests.'

Chapter Nine.

'WHERE'S SARGE?' HOLLY asked her father. Will had arrived at the hospital about an hour earlier. When Holly had snuck out for a cigarette she had expected to find Sarge tied up at his usual spot near the entrance. Today he was nowhere to be seen. Neither was Brantley.

'What do you mean? Sarge is outside,' he said, perplexed. Why was she asking? He had not long ago tied Sarge up with his own hand under Brantley's watchful eye.

'Are you sure? He wasn't there a minute ago.'

'I'll check. Wait here.'

Thirty minutes later he returned with a look of disbelief etched on his face. 'Sarge has disappeared.' He somewhat savagely swiped at his eyes with his wrists.

'What do you mean he's disappeared?'

'Brantley's gone too. They don't know where he is either.'

'What's happened?'

'Nobody knows anything. They're trying to call Brantley, but he's not answering his phone.'

'Do you think he took Sarge?'

'Sarge would never run off unless someone took him.'

'We have to find him!' Holly exclaimed, twisting her wedding rings anxiously. She glanced at her wristwatch. 'Oh, where on earth is Gilbert? I'm going outside to call him, Dad. Wait here.'

TRAFFIC WAS BACKED up on Blackfriars Bridge when Gilbert's mobile rang.

'I'm twenty minutes away,' he answered.

Holly immediately explained that Sarge had disappeared along with the hospital security guard. 'What should I do?' She sounded upset.

Gilbert's heart sank. This was precisely what he didn't need, especially given Lucy's situation. He suggested Holly might try obtaining Brantley's contact details.

Hanging up the phone, Holly marched inside to the front desk and explained to the mousey receptionist that her father's dog had vanished from outside the hospital, along with Brantley.

'I spoke to a man earlier about this. We're trying to find Brantley,' the receptionist said, sounding disinterested. Scrabbling lazily on the desk, he located a scrap of paper.

'Is your father Will Fox?'

'That's him. Could you please let us know as soon as you hear from Brantley? Sarge means the world to my dad. He's all my father has, really. Mum died a couple of years ago.' Holly was rambling.

'Write down your contact details here.' Another scrap of paper was handed to Holly, who politely requested Brantley's contact details in return.

'It's confidential.' The receptionist folded his arms.

Thinking of her father's distress, Holly mentally counted to ten. 'I assume Brantley has a boss I can talk to?'

He grudgingly located the details for the security office, his fingernail-bitten hands copying down the information.

Studying the scrap of paper and tromping down the corridor, Holly collided with somebody at a corner. 'Sorry!' she said without thinking. Looking up, she saw it was Dr Roberts.

'Whoa, slow down,' he cautioned. 'What's the rush?'

Holly paused to explain that both Brantley and Sarge had vanished. She was on a mission to speak with his boss to locate Brantley, and hopefully Sarge along with him.

'For starters, you're heading the wrong direction,' Dr Roberts said, not unkindly. 'You actually need to go back the way you came and turn left.'

Holly squinted at the small square of paper in her hand. To be honest it was difficult to decipher the scribble. Dr Roberts regarded it with irony. It looked like the handwriting of a six year old.

'Where did you get that?'

'Front desk receptionist.'

He sighed. 'I need to pick up a new ID card from the security office anyway. I'll show you the way if you like.'

'You must be dreadfully busy with your patients. I wouldn't want to trouble you.'

Dr Roberts produced a cracked, plastic identification card. 'I accidentally sat on my old one.' He pulled a face.

Holly noticed his name printed in small letters at the bottom. Dr Matthew Roberts, it said. Matthew was a nice name, she thought. She wondered if he shortened it to Matt. Holly wondered who would call him Matt; his friends and family probably, and possibly his girlfriend, too, if he had one.

Dr Roberts started moving off. She walked as fast as she could to keep up with his brisk stride.

Momentarily they arrived at the security office where he introduced her to someone called Donald. Donald was Brantley's boss and he owned a more than ample copper-hued beard. He already knew about Brantley's disappearance and was sympathetic about the missing dog. Nonetheless, Donald politely but firmly refused to furnish Holly with Brantley's contact details.

'If you give me your contact information I'll be in touch as soon as I hear anything. Unfortunately, we can't reach Brantley right now, and we don't know where he is,' Donald said, scratching his beard. 'I'm very sorry this has happened. Rest assured, we are taking this seriously, and if we don't hear from him within twenty-four hours this could become a police matter.'

Holly shivered involuntarily. That sounded ominous.

Dr Roberts collected his replacement pass while Holly supplied Donald with her information. His big hands recorded it carefully in a small, tatty-looking notebook.

Leaving the office, Holly thanked Dr Roberts. 'I think I may need a map for this place,' she added.

'People often get lost in hospitals, especially when there are other things on their minds.' He noted her tense and worried face. Buoying her up, he continued, 'I'm sure they'll find your dad's dog.' Straight eyebrows framed his eyes, which crinkled at the corners.

Holly smiled back. Somehow his words had made her feel a bit better about things.

Dr Roberts glanced at his watch. 'Heading to the sandwich shop?' He felt a bit sorry for Holly and figured some food might help cheer her up a bit.

Holly sighed. She could do with another coffee, but there was too much going on right now.

'How about tomorrow? I have to get back to Dad, and my husband is on his way, too.'

'Sounds like a plan.'

Returning to the ward, she found her father seated silently beside Lucy's bed. His eyes were squeezed shut and his lips were moving. Was he praying?

Clearing her throat she whispered, 'Dad?'

His brown eyes snapped open. 'Have you found Sarge?'

'Not yet. We'll get him back soon though. Promise.'

WHEN HER MOTHER had passed away a couple of years earlier, Holly and her father had forged a deep bond. Before then, Holly relied heavily on her mother's practical advice and support, especially when Lucy was born.

Rosalind Fox had been sanguine in nature. During her teaching days, she had been held in high regard by virtually everyone she came into contact with, on account of her practical and affable personality. She had been one of those rare people with whom others always felt comfortable—she had never been judgmental and had been unfailingly gracious. Everyone had known where they stood with Rosalind, and when she had set her mind to something, that was that. She had had steely blue eyes and an underlying resolve to match.

In the early days of Will and Rosalind's marriage, they had engaged in long, wilful battles, sometimes for days. With the arrival of Holly, they had sought to moderate their inclinations, learning as one does in the fullness of time, such struggles are really just meaningless.

Running the farm was busy work. Will had risen religiously at dawn and had retired early to bed. By circumstance and not by design, Holly hadn't seen her father every day. Whenever possible Will perched Holly on his knee, and the pair motored across the farm fields on his noisy tractor. Holly loved animals and had learned from her father how to entice the livestock close enough for her to pat them. She loved the calves and lambs, which suckled greedily at the feeding bottles she'd given them. They'd twitched their little tails and gazed at her with lash-framed eyes as they fed. Such was their enthusiasm that at times Holly had held onto the feeding bottles for dear life. As Holly had grown older, she'd begun sketching the farm beasts—graceful horses, leaping lambs, spindly-legged calves, and various other creatures that caught her eye.

With the loss of her mother Holly discovered that beyond similar appearances, she and her father were alike in other ways, too. For starters she approved of his eccentricities. Her mother would never have let him drive for miles on a tractor to the train station, whereas Holly thought it was a practical idea, not to mention somewhat amusing. Holly was a dreamer, like her father. Her regular features, toffee-coloured eyes and warm smile resembled his. They even laughed at the same things. She would shoot a glance in his direction and find similar mirth in his eyes. She respected his ways, and despite his sometimes gruff manner, she was fiercely devoted to him. So was Lucy, who loved to spend time with him and Gloria on the farm.

'YOU MADE IT!' Holly hugged her husband, who eventually turned up, forty minutes later. Gilbert greeted his father-in-law, who acknowledged him with a frown. Will was still thinking about Sarge.

Gilbert cleared his throat. 'Sorry I'm late; traffic was a nightmare. How is Lucy today?'

'She's okay. Dr Roberts seems to think everything is progressing the right way.'

Holly watched Gilbert gently stroke Lucy's small hand. Squeezing his arm, she looked at him affectionately. 'It's good to see you.'

Will muttered something about the bathroom and excused himself from the ward.

'Sarge is still missing,' Holly explained.

'I'm sure he'll turn up,' Gilbert said reassuringly. 'He can't have gone far.' He changed the subject. 'I have a book for Lucy I was planning to read her.' He pulled it from his coat pocket, and Holly saw it was the latest in Lucy's favourite series.

Will returned momentarily, still frowning.

'Any sign of Sarge?' Gilbert asked him.

'Nope.'

Holly weighed things up. 'Dad, perhaps you might like to stay over at Larkspur?' Thinking of an excuse for him to stay, she added, 'I need to call a couple of gallery owners tonight. It's a long drive and I could do with the company to stay awake.'

Will knew exactly what his daughter was up to and for once he didn't argue. He had finally started to enjoy life a little more after Rosalind's death. Frankly, the thought of returning home without Sarge filled him with an inexplicable dread.

'If you insist,' he agreed.

Gilbert gazed intently at his wife. He was crestfallen. He had been looking forward to spending time with Holly at the apartment. He supposed the extra sleep would be nice at least.

Later on, Holly kissed her husband goodbye.

'Text me when you arrive home safely,' Gilbert said.

Holly saw the disappointment in his eyes. 'I'll stay at the apartment with you tomorrow night. Promise,' she whispered, gently squeezing Gilbert's hand.

GLORIA HYTHE ANSWERED the phone with her usual greeting. 'Fox residence,' she said in a clear voice, not expecting the reply that boomed down the receiver.

'This is Tilda Wright. Are you the owner of Sarge?'

Gloria was perplexed. 'No, but the owner lives here. He isn't available right now though. Could I help?'

'I believe Sarge is missing from his owner.' Aunty Tilda fidgeted with the handset. 'We found him. He's with us.'

Missing? This was the first Gloria heard of it. Quick as blink she replied, 'You'd better give me your telephone number, and I'll get Mr Fox to call you right back.'

Gloria then phoned Will on his mobile. She wasn't certain where he was right now and was pretty sure he hadn't come home last night either. This was a good reason for her to check up on things.

'Will Fox,' he answered with his gruff voice.

'Will, it's Gloria.' She got straight to the point. 'Have you lost Sarge?'

'How did you know…has he turned up at home?'

'No, he hasn't. Someone named Tilda Wright phoned about him. She wants you to phone her back. It sounds as if she has him.'

'Is he alive?'

'I'm not sure,' Gloria said. 'Is everything okay?'

'Just give me the number. I'll tell you everything soon.' Scribbling it down, Will hurriedly disengaged himself from Gloria's well-meaning but somewhat irksome questions. He had a call to make, and he didn't like the suspense.

Aunty Tilda was expecting a call from Sarge's owner. She answered straight away with an anticipative tone in her big voice.

When Will heard Sarge was alive, his heart leapt for joy.

'Alive and well! Where is he now?'

'Safe with me,' Aunty Tilda answered after a small pause. 'In Leeds.'

'Leeds?' he echoed. 'How did he get there?'

She sighed heavily. 'It's probably best if all this is explained tomorrow. My nephew will be returning him to you at the hospital.'

Everything clicked into place. 'Your nephew is—Brantley?'

'Yes.'

'Is everything alright with the boy?'

Aunty Tilda was not one to mince words, even painful ones. 'The boy lost his mother very suddenly. Stroke.'

'I am sorry.'

'I'm dealing with him.'

Will wisely probed no more and arrangements were made for Sarge to be returned tomorrow at 3 p.m. sharp. This would take place outside the hospital, at the entrance.

True to Aunty Tilda's word, Brantley was punctual. Upon spying his master, Sarge escaped Brantley's grip. With a loud bark, Sarge bounded joyfully into Will's open arms. He licked Will and wagged his tail so furiously that his furry hindquarters shook with the momentum.

Holly observed the happy reunion. She knew how attached her father was to Sarge, and his unabashed delight was really rather touching.

'Hi,' Brantley said tentatively. He nervously pulled his fingers. The joints cracked.

She appraised him coolly. 'Hi.'

'Me mam died,' he burst out. 'I didn't mean to take the dog. I panicked and ran. I know I shouldn't have and I'm here to make things right.'

Brantley looked miserably at the concrete. He had seen her type before—expensive clothes, fancy cars, breezing in and out of the hospital with all the time in the world at their disposal and all wrapped up in their spiffy selves.

Holly was disarmed by this revelation and took a drag of her cigarette.

'I'm sorry,' she said at last. Not knowing what else to say, she enquired, 'Are you okay?'

'The funeral is tomorrow.' He rubbed his throbbing temples. 'Look, when I heard about me mam, I was out here see, on the job. Me Aunty Tilda phoned out of the blue and told me what happened. I did some dumb things, made some errors of judgment.'

Looking downcast, he continued. 'When Aunty Tilda heard I left my post and took the dog she was angry.' His words trailed off.

Holly stated the facts. 'You left your post without telling your boss.' Without intending to she sounded incredulous.

'I didn't mean to.' Brantley looked crestfallen. 'Truth be told I was thinking only about me mam and nothing else. I know it's no excuse. It was a dumb thing to do.'

Will was by now on his feet. He had heard the entire story. 'No harm done, son,' he said with his usual good humour.

Holly warily evaluated the doleful Brantley and then observed Sarge, still jubilantly wagging his tail. Lastly she studied her father. A load was lifted from his shoulders and his brown eyes were once more hopeful and twinkling.

Squeezing his daughter's shoulder, he said, 'All's well that ends well. Sarge is back isn't he? Brantley made a mistake and he's putting things right.' Pausing, he added, 'The lad just lost his mother. You know how that feels.'

At once Holly felt a pang. How could she forget losing her mum? Her father's forgiving nature never ceased to amaze her, in fact it was one of the things she loved best about him.

'I gotta talk to Donald,' Brantley said, interrupting her train of thought.

'Wait!' Holly said. 'I'll come with you. I need to speak with him, too.'

Brantley looked perplexed, but nodded meekly. 'Ok.' He hoped this didn't mean Holly was about to land him in even more hot water.

101

DONALD WAS ON the phone when Brantley and Holly approached, and his big hands nearly dropped the receiver. 'Something's come up, gotta go,' he said, hurriedly ending the call.

'Well?' he asked through his bushy beard, inspecting Brantley with a distinctly unimpressed expression on his face. He had been expecting Brantley, thanks to a rather intriguing phone call from Tilda Wright, who had outlined the details and assured him that Brantley would be appearing tomorrow to explain himself and offer an apology.

Brantley opened his mouth to speak, but Holly cut in.

'I apologise for interrupting.' She shot a look at Brantley, which made him close his mouth. 'I want to say something in Brantley's defence. He knows it was wrong to er…disappear. He's here now—the day before his mother's funeral—to put things right.'

Both Brantley and Donald gaped at her. Despite his imposing appearance, Donald was not an unfair man. He surveyed his employee's dejected appearance, and not without sympathy.

'Where is the missing dog?'

'We found him.' Holly cleared her throat and quickly changed the subject. 'Look, I know how it feels to lose a mother.' Her voice dropped an octave. 'Brantley lost his mum very suddenly and I ask, Mr Donald, that with this in mind, you would be lenient with him. That's all.'

Donald nodded gravely. 'Could you please give us a moment, Miss, er, Holly?'

Turning to go, Holly nearly collided with Dr Roberts, who had materialised at the doorway.

'I'm terribly sorry,' he said. 'I seem to have this bad habit of running into you at corners.'

Holly shot a look over her shoulder at Brantley and Donald. 'You might want to come back in a couple of minutes.' She wore a relieved smile.

They stepped out of the room. On cue, the security office door closed after them.

Dr Roberts looked at Holly with a strange expression in his eyes. 'I'm sorry, but I couldn't help overhearing what just happened. Did your dad's dog turn up?'

'Sure did; he's back.' Remembering her dad was waiting outside with Sarge, she added, 'Actually, I have to go. See you back at the ward.'

Pacing off, she left Dr Roberts staring after her. Turning down the corridor she looked back and gave a small wave. He was still gazing after her.

OUTSIDE THE MAIN entrance of the hospital, she found her father discussing what had happened with Gilbert, who she greeted with a kiss.

'So who was this Donald person you went to see?' Gilbert enquired as he embraced his wife.

Holly explained what had just taken place and Gilbert's eyes glinted with unintended pleasure. One of the things he loved best about Holly was her kind heart. Compared to the hard-nosed corporate world of banking, he had always found it somewhat refreshing.

'I'm glad Sarge is back,' he said with relief. Glancing at his wristwatch, he asked, 'Coming to see Lucy?'

Will cleared his throat. 'I'll be off. I'll be back in the morning.' Whipping a lead from his pocket, he deftly attached it to Sarge's collar. 'See you. Think I'll leave the dog at home tomorrow.'

After hugging Will and saying goodbye, Gilbert and Holly made their way into the hospital together, complete with Holly's overnight bag.

Chapter Ten.

EARLY THE NEXT morning, Holly left the still-sleeping Gilbert and quietly crept from the apartment. There was no denying that, following recent events, Gilbert was shattered. His workload continued to be demanding. Last night, they had fallen asleep as soon as their heads hit the pillows. There was a problem, however. Holly was continually waking in the small hours of the morning, and unable to get back to sleep. She would toss and turn for hours while she waited for the sun to come up. She worried about Lucy and everything else in the world worth worrying about. After a few nights of this, she understood why sleep deprivation was an effective instrument of torture. Her eyes were bloodshot, and at times, she could hear a buzzing sound in her ears.

At the hospital, she purchased a black coffee from the cafeteria. She made her way to Lucy's ward with the cup carefully balanced in her small hand. Lucy was still in her usual state, comatose on the sterile hospital bed, surrounded by tubes and machines, with the ever-present nurse nearby.

'Hello, darling.' Holly gently kissed the smooth tip of her daughter's nose. She sipped at the sweet, scalding coffee, and savoured the temporary quietness of the London morning. Outside she could hear pigeons cooing.

Soon enough, Dr Roberts appeared for Lucy's regular check-up.

'Bright and early again.' He greeted Holly with a warm smile as he strode into the ward.

'Good morning,' she replied. 'How are you?'

'Fine thanks. Your father must be relieved to have his dog back.'

'Absolutely. He loves that animal. Gloria gave it to him when Mum died. Gloria is Dad's housekeeper.' Holly sighed and tiredly rubbed her temples. 'Too much information,' she said apologetically.

'It's okay.' Changing the subject, he said, 'Sorry for eavesdropping yesterday.' He fiddled with his sleeve. 'I was actually picking up my new ID card. The one I was given the other day was just temporary while I was waiting for my new one.'

'Oh,' Holly said, not quite knowing what to say.

'What you did was kind. Not many people would do that.' His gaze met hers. Holly looked away and adjusted a small diamond stud her ear. Dr Roberts cleared his throat. 'Actually, I need to discuss next steps for Lucy. Would you like to do that now—or perhaps wait until your husband and father are here also?'

'Is everything alright?'

'Seems to be. It would be good to discuss Lucy's condition when you have a minute. She's nearly ready to come out of her coma.'

At that moment, Will strolled in with a brown paper bag. It contained freshly baked gingerbread from Gloria, who by now was fully briefed on Sarge's situation. Holly greeted him with a hug.

'Dr Roberts was just explaining how Lucy is almost ready to be woken up,' she said.

Will nodded sagely and looked around the ward. 'Where's Gilbert?'

'Just catching some extra sleep. He'll be here later.'

'Good morning, Will,' Dr Roberts said.

Will returned the greeting. He looked decidedly more chipper today.

Dr Roberts looked questioningly at Holly, who nodded. Clearing his throat, he began, 'As you know we used sedatives to put Lucy's brain into hibernation. We needed to reduce the swelling and pressure to allow it to rest. She's responded well, so we're going to start weaning her from the sedatives, and from there, we'll begin neurological testing to determine the extent of the damage.'

Upon hearing the word *damage*, Holly's heart began thumping erratically against her ribcage. It had been doing that often lately. She took deep breaths to calm down.

'Damage?' she repeated, feeling a little sick.

'There's no denying Lucy took a serious knock to her head.' Dr Roberts tone was grave. 'Initially there didn't appear to be any obvious damage, but her situation was so borderline that when she was admitted here it was necessary to protect her brain from secondary injury, which is sometimes more damaging than the initial injury.'

Dr Roberts stopped what he was saying and stared at Holly. 'Are you alright?'

Holly was doing some deep breathing, steadily in and out, as instructed when she had conducted an internet search for her mysterious 'heart attacks,' which in fact appeared to be anxiety attacks.

'I think it's anxiety,' she panted.

'Put your head between your knees,' Dr Roberts instructed. Placing one hand on her back he gently helped her do it. 'There, you're doing great.'

In a few moments, Holly's heartbeat regulated. She sat up. Her father and Dr Roberts both stared at her with a good measure of concern.

'Have you had any breakfast?' Dr Roberts asked.

'Not really.' Holly confessed, embarrassed. She had been skipping breakfast so she could spend more time with Lucy.

Will offered her a ginger biscuit, which she crunched into gratefully. Feeling slightly dizzy, fatigue washed over her in waves. Tilting her head back, she closed her eyes.

'You should get some rest, Holly,' Dr Roberts said. 'You're overdoing it.'

To her mortification, a tear escaped from her right eye and slid down her cheek.

'Take it easy,' her father chimed in. 'Perhaps you should go back to Gilbert's apartment for some shut eye?'

Opening her eyes, Holly took a breath and rubbed her face. 'No, I'm fine. I just...didn't realise how tired I was, that's all.' She brushed an errant biscuit crumb from her dress. 'No need to make a fuss, honestly.'

Dr Roberts had seen this before, people who felt they must appear strong in the face of adversity. Inevitably their emotions leaked and were manifest in any number of ways. You name it, he had seen it all. He had originally pegged Holly as the spoiled, rich type. Pleasant enough, just shallow, he'd thought. Smoothing his rather overgrown blonde hair, he briefly squeezed Holly's shoulder. His grey eyes were filled with concern.

'You just press the buzzer if you need anything, Holly.' His opinion of her had changed yesterday when he had overheard her defending Brantley. It was easy to hold grudges when wronged, then nurse and pursue them. Holly could easily have given Brantley a piece of her mind and demanded he be fired. In fact, it was probably quite within her rights to do so. In his experience, most people were ready to sue anyone given half the chance. They did it for various reasons—it was expected of them, for profit, for revenge, or they just liked the drama. It was refreshing to meet somebody so contrary to the pedestrian, to the everyday and predictable. Holly was different—remarkable, but married. He respected that. Nonetheless, she was someone he knew he could be friends with given half the chance, someone who could perhaps sharpen his world view by just being themselves.

Being a doctor afforded him a myriad of interesting insights into the human condition. Privately he thought Gilbert was a bit, well...intense, whereas Holly was young and insouciant. In some ways they seemed a mismatched couple, he thought, but obviously it worked for them.

Striding from the ward, he brushed these thoughts from his mind and continued with his rounds.

HOLLY STEPPED TIREDLY through the door of the apartment. She expected Gilbert would be on his way to the hospital, which would leave her to uninterrupted sleep. Instead, she discovered him on the phone in the spare room, which was set up as a study. Waving to her, he mouthed something indecipherable. Holly retreated to the sitting room, where she scribbled a note that said:

Please do not disturb—wife needs sleep. x

She placed it on the heavy, glass-topped coffee table, and stumbled into the main bedroom, where she stripped to her underwear and crawled into Gilbert's bed. Slumber soon claimed her. Sometime later, she awoke to the sound of a key scraping in the door. Rubbing her eyes, she wobbled into the sitting room. Outside it was dark, and in the distance a few brightly lit barges slid along the muddy Thames River. Traffic roared distantly outside. Gilbert was holding paper carry bags, from which wafted the delicious aroma of hot Vietnamese food.

'Hello,' he said, gazing appreciatively at Holly's slim figure.

Bypassing Gilbert's admiring stare, she sleepily returned his greeting.

'Hungry?'

Her stomach growled. 'Actually, I am.' The food smelled great. 'I'll get plates.' She moved to the open-plan dining area and began laying the table.

'Dr Roberts told me what happened to you earlier.' Gilbert's shoulders were tense. 'Are you okay?'

'I'm fine,' Holly waved it off with a small smile. 'Overtiredness and worry got the better of me.' She placed a fork carefully on the table. 'How was Lucy today?'

'She's fine. Dr Roberts will begin bringing Lucy from her coma tomorrow.'

'I know.' Her stomach knotted once more. 'Did he tell you about the uh, damage?'

'Holly—' he put his arms around her. 'She'll be okay. Everything has gone to plan so far. You know how doctors are; they always explain the risks and worse case scenarios.'

'I know.' Holly sighed. 'It's just been so—' she rubbed her eyes and searched for the right word. 'Intense.'

Gilbert began unloading containers of hot food from the bags onto the Italian dining table. 'Shall we eat before it gets cold?'

Holly sat as Gilbert spooned tasty looking food on porcelain dinner plates. She speared a prawn with one of her chopsticks.

'As long as you're okay, Holly—I don't know what I'd do if anything happened to you.'

'I know, Gilbert,' she whispered. 'I know.'

THE NEXT MORNING, the sun was up in a cloudless and pale blue sky. With a feeling of optimism, Holly slipped out to collect fresh croissants from a nearby bakery along with a morning newspaper. Back at the apartment, she brewed a pot of strong coffee just as Gilbert liked it. Awakened by its pleasing aroma, he padded to the kitchen and sleepily kissed his wife good morning.

Chewing and sipping companionably, Holly casually asked, 'When are you heading off to New York?

'Tuesday.' With a furrowed brow, Gilbert was examining the business pages. Looking up at her with a concerned expression in his blue-green eyes he enquired, 'Will you be alright?'

'I'll survive.' Today was Friday, which meant Gilbert would be leaving in four days' time.

'When will you be back?' she asked.

'In a couple of weeks.'

Holly smiled. Despite the circumstances, at least she was getting to spend more time with Gilbert than normal. She liked that.

LUCY EMERGED FROM her coma and remembered nothing at all about the accident. Curiously, she recalled her coma as if it were a dream. In fact, she referred to angels being at her bedside. Gilbert was around to see his daughter groggily awaken. With a lighter heart and a spring in his step he boarded his plane for New York, and his unfinished business meetings. For the sake of convenience, Holly stayed on at the apartment and provided Gilbert with daily updates on Lucy's rather encouraging progress.

Holly knew she was out of touch with Gilbert's life, as he was with hers. Gilbert's apartment was modern and spartan, and she decided to surprise him with a few homely touches here and there. She paid a visit to a nearby department store and bought a colourful Turkish throw for the sofa. For added flourish, she would introduce some of her paintings to the neutral walls. Perhaps when Lucy was fully recovered they might return to the apartment for family days out. Daydreaming of the things they might do together—outings at London's zoo, lunch at nearby cafés, picnics at Hyde Park—she hummed and smoothed the patterned throw on the sofa.

Chapter Eleven.

HOLLY'S CELLPHONE TRILLED.

'Hello, darling!' Tammy's tone was dry. 'I'm still at work. Can you believe it?' She was often so busy that she resorted to texting instead of speaking.

Holly was surprised by the phone call. She knew the long hours Tammy worked at her busy advertising agency. An idea occurred to her. 'Guess where I am?'

'Having afternoon tea with Prince Charles? I give up; where are you?'

'At Gilbert's apartment while Lucy's in hospital. We should catch up, it's been forever.'

'I'm free tonight after work, as a matter of fact. Is Lucy okay?'

'It looks like there's no brain damage. She'll be out of hospital soon.' Holly twisted a strand of her hair around her forefinger. 'Her spine will take more time to heal, but she'll be able to rest and recover at home.'

'Blimey. You'd better give me all the details tonight. Any hot doctor's at the hospital?' It was a throwaway question and Tammy was surprised when her friend hesitated before answering.

'I'm a married woman, I'll have you know. Actually, Lucy's doctor has been amazing.'

Sensing there was more to this than met the eye, Tammy suggested they meet at a sleek steak restaurant in central London.

After showering Holly pulled on her favourite black

trousers, which went with everything. She had bought them at Bloomingdales in New York a year ago, the one and only time she had tagged along on one of Gilbert's business trips. While there, she barely saw him and amused herself with sightseeing and a spot of shopping. Rummaging through her suitcase she located a brand new, off-the-shoulder top—a hastily packed addition prior to leaving Larkspur. Holly slipped it on and then spritzed some rose perfume on her wrists. A mirror inspection revealed her thick russet tresses didn't look quite right. The shampoo Gilbert kept at the apartment had made her hair static and flyaway. Time was running out and she was due at the restaurant in forty-five minutes. Holly hated being late for anything. Others might not mind but she did. Twisting her hair back, she secured it with hairpins, slipped into a pair of heels, applied lip gloss and a dash of mascara, and then grabbed her Mulberry handbag. Still humming, she locked the apartment door behind her, and caught the elevator to the ground floor, where a taxi was waiting.

'WHICH STEAK WOULD you like?' A gigantic grey slate platter was hoisted under Tammy's nose by the wiry waitress. It was almost a third of her height in length, matched her body width and was covered with carefully sliced slabs of raw beef.

With a hungry look in her eye, Tammy made a quick decision and Holly followed suit. Tammy then asked the waitress for a bottle of champagne.

'It's been too long hasn't it?' She spread her gleaming red fingernails on the immaculate table-top.

'Yep.' Holly grinned. 'Now, spill the beans on all the gossip. I want details please.'

'Wait a minute! Who's this hunky doctor looking after Lucy?' Tammy fixed her gaze on Holly.

The champagne arrived and was popped open. Two frothy flutes were filled. Holly took a thirsty mouthful and the bubbles pinged on her tongue.

'Trust you.' Holly chuckled. 'Lucy calls him Gabriel.' She glanced shyly at Tammy. 'I suppose he is rather handsome. But it's not like that—we've had coffee a couple of times, that's all. He's good to talk to.'

Tammy cocked an eyebrow under her dark and heavy Gallic-looking fringe. Before she could dig any deeper Holly continued speaking. She relayed events—Lucy's accident, her coma, recovery thus far, and her time with Gilbert at the apartment. The words tumbled out. She spoke of Sarge's abduction and subsequent reappearance, along with Brantley and Aunty Tilda's involvement.

The waitress deftly refilled the flutes. The girls clinked glasses. 'To Lucy,' they said.

Holly inspected the delicate flute in her hand. 'These bubbles have gone straight to my head. Sometimes I forget to eat,' she confessed.

Tammy nodded. She had cupids bow lips, azure blue eyes and long, curled lashes, which she batted constantly. People often wondered if they were real. Holly knew they were one hundred percent real, and Tammy used them to full effect.

'I know it probably wasn't funny at the time,' Tammy said, suppressing a giggle and wriggling out of her vintage Chanel jacket. 'But fancy the hospital security guard abducting your dad's dog! Who does that?'

She gestured to the waitress, who hurried over.

'Can we have some cheesy bread please?' She shot a look in Holly's direction and winked. 'My friend needs to eat something, fast.'

Holly giggled and took another sip of champagne. 'Actually you couldn't make it up if you tried. The sad part was poor Brantley's mum died very suddenly so he just upped and left his job—with Sarge. Dad was devastated. It was the last straw really.' Holly stopped and swallowed. 'Actually it was horrendous, Tammy,' she said soberly.

'I know.' Tammy squeezed her friend's arm. The warm cheesy bread duly arrived, and the girls munched on the soft, comforting dough.

'Your turn to spill the beans. What's been happening in the glamorous and fast-paced world of media?'

'Trust me, it isn't as glamorous as it appears.' Tammy wrinkled her pretty nose. 'Some of my clients are really ungrateful. At least I get plenty of lunch offers from media owners who want to sell me advertising space on their websites. I'm piggy in the middle getting fat on a permanent champagne diet.' She pinched a minuscule piece of flesh on her midriff, sighed and gulped her champagne. 'I'm tired. I work late every night. My phone rings incessantly and I'm plugged into my emails twenty-four seven. Unless I know the number I don't answer calls, but sometimes I make the terrible mistake of picking up and regretting it immediately when I hear the desperate voice of a media owner who's been stalking me for days, wanting to be my best friend so they can sell me advertising space I probably don't need. You can practically hear their sales targets crunching.'

Tammy glanced at her phone, but chose to ignore the tiny flashing light that signalled a message was waiting for her. Instead, she took another slug of champagne and inspected the almost-empty bottle.

'Fancy a cocktail?' she asked mischievously. 'I need to blow off some steam.'

Signalling for service, the girls ordered two mojitos and the obliging waitress sped off. She sensed a good tip coming from this table. Customers who drank plenty tended to be generous.

Tammy changed the subject. 'There's this guy in the office I'm sort of seeing—'

'Go on.' Holly encouraged. Tales of her friend's love life were often hugely entertaining.

As it happened Tammy was seeing the agency heartthrob, named Adam, who now appeared to be flirting with a pretty grad who had joined the agency just six weeks earlier. Problem was he had just the type of smile and defined forearms that girls found irresistible.

'I knew from the beginning he was a lothario.' Tammy shrugged.

After a few cocktails and a lot of steak, the girls happily stumbled from the restaurant. The waitress beamed at their retreating backs as she gathered the extra cash from the silver tipping dish and pocketed it. These sorts of customers effectively doubled her hourly wage and made her job worthwhile.

On the pavement the girls swayed gently in the warm evening air.

'There's a media haunt nearby,' Tammy ventured. 'Get this, called *Promised Land*. Wanna check it out? It's media night tonight. It'll be a hoot.'

Holly looked blankly at Tammy.

'Basically it means media owners will be out in droves,' Tammy explained. 'With open wallets, falling over themselves to impress ad-agency peeps like me with free booze and getting hammered on their company credit cards. Things can get messy when we fraternise,' she added cheerfully.

'What's a media owner?'

'Well, for me it's people from media companies who sell internet advertising space of some description.'

Holly hesitated. To be honest it was not really her thing. She was more accustomed to understated gatherings at swanky art exhibitions. Besides, she planned to be at the hospital first thing tomorrow morning. Still, it had been months since she had last seen Tammy, and Holly was reluctant to let the night slip from her grip too readily.

'Sure. Just one drink. Then I have to get some beauty sleep.' A thought occurred to her: 'Why don't you visit me and Lucy at the hospital tomorrow? That is, if you can escape the office and that hunky lothario.'

Tammy saluted. 'By hook or by crook, I'll be there.'

A short trek later and they arrived at *Promised Land*, which lived up to Tammy's vivid description. It heaved with achingly trendy media types who periodically broke into uproarious laughter, accompanied by vigorous back slapping. Dimly lit Moroccan lamps were chained to the ceiling and swayed to the thumping pop music. Soon enough, Tammy was approached by a purposeful looking man and woman, dressed in sexy, corporate attire. The man had on a tight pale pink shirt, and his hair swirled this way and that way. The woman was a blonde bombshell with legs up to her armpits. She wore a super short skirt that showed off her potential. The woman bestowed effusive air kisses all around with her shiny red lips.

'Media owners,' Tammy hissed knowingly to Holly. 'From an internet advertising network.' Snapping her fingers, she tried to remember who they were, but failed. 'I forget their names.'

Presently, drinks offers were made. Holly opted for a gin and tonic. Tammy took a large Rioja.

Small talk was being made, but Holly could barely hear the words over the music. Something called 'click through rates' was being discussed, whatever that was.

During the course of the conversation, she learned the media owners names were Amber and Russell. When she was halfway through her drink Russell looked at her enquiringly and pointed to her glass. 'Refill?'

Holly shook her head. 'No, thank you.'

Noticing Tammy's wine was already gone, Russell made his way to the busy bar and returned with another round of drinks, carefully balanced in his hands. Positioning himself by Holly, he handed them out. Taking a swig of lager, he fixed her with a blue-eyed stare and asked, 'So where do you work?' This question was unashamedly designed to figure out Holly's usefulness. If she worked for an advertising agency the ensuing questions would ascertain whether she was worth sucking up to.

Briefly Holly contemplated the crunching sales targets Tammy had referred to earlier over dinner.

'I'm an artist,' she replied.

Russell's face fell. He took another mouthful of beer and asked a few polite questions about her vocation, all of which Holly answered patiently. Obviously he knew very little about the art world. Holly contemplated the strange swirling pattern of Russell's carefully gelled hair. It reminded her a little of the ocean. For a second she thought about painting a sea-scape and then checked her wristwatch. It was half past eleven. Unless she left soon it was going to be a real struggle getting up early to go to the hospital.

'I must get going,' she said politely. 'It was, er, nice to meet you.'

Russell fished for something in the slim-line pocket of his perfectly fitted shirt. 'Here's my business card.' With one hand he passed it to her while the other snaked round and squeezed her behind.

Startled, Holly let go of the card, which fluttered to the murky floor. She didn't pick it up.

'I'm married,' she snapped, pointing to her ring finger. 'Mar-ried!'

Russell shrugged. 'Yes,' he replied, gazing hopefully at her with baby blue eyes. 'But are you happy?'

For a moment, Holly wasn't sure if he was serious. She scrutinised his sticky hair and carefully scrubbed face and realised he probably was. Holly propelled herself in Tammy's direction and almost knocked the drink from her friend's hand.

'I have to go,' she hissed into Tammy's ear. 'Russell just grabbed my butt. Better make a move before he turns into an octopus and I slap him.'

'Wait,' Tammy said. 'I'm coming too.'

Before long, the girls were in the cooling night air. Fortunately at this hour, there were usually plenty of taxis whirring about the streets, on the hunt for fares. Presently, four minicabs approached in quick succession all open for business.

As they were driven through the late-night city streets

towards their respective destinations, Tammy realised she had forgotten to get details about the intriguing Dr Roberts. She resolved to visit the hospital at lunchtime tomorrow no matter what landed on her work desk. From eight years of age, she and Holly had been best friends. It was difficult having secrets from each other; their friendship was far too established for that. Media could be fickle and shallow, and Holly's friendship meant the world to her.

As Tammy reclined in the taxi's back seat she contemplated something that had been on her mind a lot lately—the merits of a younger boyfriend. Younger men were more, well, malleable. Apparently some of them even preferred experienced older women to the fledgling feminine variety. Tammy smiled at the prospects. Sod the office lothario, she thought. Time for something and someone new. She would write her own rule book.

'I'll have a cougar experience,' she resolved.

Chapter Twelve.

'HELLO, STRANGER.' DR Roberts smiled broadly at Holly when he strode into the ward early the next morning. She certainly was an early riser. 'Feeling better?'

'Much improved,' Holly replied. She smiled back, steaming coffee in hand, as usual.

'Morning, Gabriel,' Lucy piped from her pillow.

'Morning, Lucy,' Dr Roberts said, his eyes sparkling. There was nothing more gratifying than a patient who responded well. Patients in similar situations could be extremely delicate and some did not respond well at all. In fact some didn't recover from their comas or they stayed in them for longer than intended.

He briskly checked Lucy's patient file, which had been updated just a moment ago by a solemn-looking nurse.

'You're almost ready to go home, my dear. Would you like that?'

Gently he rubbed Lucy's scalp where the stitches from her injury had been removed. 'These are healing nicely,' he remarked. 'Your hair will grow back in no time.'

Lucy's scalp had been shaved shortly after arriving at hospital to allow the medical staff to better examine and treat her injuries. Although Lucy was on the mend there was no denying the toll her accident had taken on her body. She was still pale, thin and in places, bruised.

'Lots more rest for you, my dear,' Dr Roberts said.

Lucy listened intently to all of this. 'Am I looking

forward to going home?' She repeated his earlier question. Contemplating her answer, she replied, 'Yes and no.'

'Wait a minute! You're the first patient of mine who actually wants to stay in this old place! What's wrong with you?'

Lucy chortled. 'I like the angels here.'

Dr Roberts shot an amused glance at Holly. 'I'm sure there are also angels at home.'

'When will she be ready to go home?' Holly asked. With a pang she realised that her contact with Dr Roberts was drawing to an end. She had grown to enjoy his down-to-earth personality.

'Give it another week,' Dr Roberts said. 'She's doing remarkably well, but is still a bit, well, fragile,' he chose his words carefully. 'One more week and she can go. But plenty more rest is needed. Her injuries are still healing.'

Holly nodded gravely. She was under no illusion as to how fortunate Lucy had been to recover even this fast.

'HOW'S THE HEAD?' Holly squashed a cigarette with her heel as Tammy strolled towards her.

'Fine, thanks,' Tammy replied. 'Just a bit tired.'

Meeting outside the hospital was the easiest option. Once inside its labyrinth of highly polished linoleum corridors, it was all too easy to become disorientated. There was no sign of Brantley. A different security guard loomed silently beside the large glass sliding doors, on the lookout for any signs of danger. Holly wondered what had become of Brantley and whether she should return to the security office to enquire.

The girls embraced. 'By the way, I dumped Adam this morning,' Tammy remarked.

'Good for you!' Holly replied. 'How did it go?'

'I sent him an email.'

Holly rolled her eyes. She recalled Tammy's dumping of a different, unwanted office boyfriend six months earlier. Tammy had created an email calendar reminder simply saying, *Dump Brad.* The reminder popped up on her laptop at a team meeting during a presentation she was giving. Poor Brad spotted it, as did everybody else in the room. He stormed out with a red-face, refused to speak to Tammy for weeks afterwards and requested that he be moved to another team within the agency. Fortunately, he eventually saw the funny side of the matter, and somehow, they even managed to remain friends. Tammy was one of those rare people who possessed an uncanny knack for remaining on good terms with her many ex-boyfriends. Holly sometimes wondered how she did it.

Holly linked arms with Tammy and guided her to Lucy's ward. 'She dozes quite a lot,' Holly whispered, stroking Lucy's shorn head.

'Poor poppet.' Tammy squeezed Holly's hand. 'I'm so glad she's on the mend.'

'One more week and I'll be able to take her home.' Holly wore a small smile as she said this.

Dr Roberts entered the ward for his usual rounds. Spotting Holly, he strode over.

'Don't worry if she sleeps often.' He briefly checked his notes. 'It's all part of the healing process.'

Tammy gazed on with interest thinking that Dr Roberts was very dishy indeed. As if reading her mind, Holly introduced them, giving Tammy a pointed look as she did so. As they shook hands Dr Roberts carefully eyed Tammy, noting her tailored black trousers, her cream silk shirt, and shiny high-heeled ankle boots.

'Little Lucy here is making a remarkable recovery.' He rubbed his chin. 'She's doing very well indeed.'

'I'm so glad.' Tammy beamed, batting her especially mascaraed eyelashes. 'I'm sure being looked after by you also helps. Holly tells me Lucy refers to you as Gabriel.'

Dr Roberts gave a bemused smile. 'It certainly helps to have a supportive family onsite.' He adjusted a shirt cuff, which had unrolled itself.

Tammy eyed his defined forearms with interest. Who

needed media boys? They were so, well, metro. Furthermore, some of them used more hairspray and facial scrub than she did. She made a mental note to date more men from other walks of life.

'I'll be back in a bit,' Dr Roberts said, tucking a pen into the pocket of his white coat. 'Have you considered escaping to the outside world for some lunch? Don't worry, I'll keep an eye on Lucy.'

Holly looked reluctant.

'Go on,' he pressed with a smile. 'It will do you good. There's that fantastic sandwich shop around the corner, which also makes a mean coffee.' He nodded reassuringly at Holly. 'Lucy will be fine.'

'Come on, Holly,' Tammy said, remembering that last night over dinner Holly had confessed she was forgetting to eat.

The girls stepped outside and into a city that had been transformed by a couple of weeks of sunshine. Londoners had broken out with uncharacteristic smiles, and even sunglasses. In the parks they exposed their pasty limbs to the sun's rays. Altogether, summer had a cheering effect on everyone. Holly and Tammy giggled and ordered sandwiches from a jolly Scottish woman, who relentlessly bestowed an imaginative repertoire of pet names upon her queuing customers. Then, amid sun-seeking bodies at a nearby park, they munched their sandwiches.

'These are superb,' Holly remarked through a mouthful of focaccia and salmon.

'So is Dr Roberts,' Tammy replied.

Holy spotted the mischievous glint in Tammy's eyes and her heart sank. She wasn't even sure why. After all, she was married and Dr Roberts's love life was no business of hers. She supposed it was because she felt some kind of bond with him over Lucy's ordeal. She had enjoyed their chats over coffee and didn't want Tammy manhandling him, even though she was her best friend.

'Is he single?' Tammy asked.

'How would I know?' Holly said crossly. Then she immediately apologised. 'Sorry, Tammy. It's just that I consider him a friend of sorts.' Swallowing her mouthful she continued, 'It's silly really—I guess I've become attached because of Lucy. He's just very decent you know? Not that you're not,' Holly hastened to add, her eyes earnest.

Tammy reflected how her friend's eyes always seemed to darken a shade during particularly intense moments, from toffee to fudge. She nodded thoughtfully. It seemed Holly had developed a crush on the delectable Dr Roberts, which meant he was a no-go area.

By today's standards, Tammy was a thoroughly modern woman. Some might say that she was a notorious flirt. She would happily make a play for this Dr Roberts, or should she say, Matt, if Holly—despite being married—were not in the way. She sighed. Best friends came first no matter what. Then, remembering her cougar plans, she instantly cheered up.

SCRATCHING HIS AMPLE beard, which when the temperature rose became itchy, Donald considered what to do about the Brantley situation. That remarkable woman's intervention had cast doubt on his usual instincts, which were to fire him on the spot.

Right now, Brantley was on special leave with his family in Leeds, legitimately this time. He would be back in a few days and then Donald would decide what to do with him. It wasn't ideal leaving things at loose ends. But, given the extraordinary circumstances, it was the least he could do without feeling like an ogre.

GILBERT RETURNED TO London a couple of weeks later as planned. He noticed Holly's decorative touches in the apartment. It was sweet of her to take an interest in his life outside Larkspur, something she rarely did. Being absent from home for long periods of time wasn't ideal; he knew that. You'd have to be a fool not to recognise that wives needed maintenance, which was why he took pride in his gift-buying abilities. Lucy's accident had gone some way towards bringing him and Holly closer together and he was grateful for that, even though it wasn't easy.

It occurred to Gilbert that perhaps time—that elusive and valuable commodity—was the answer to Holly's discontent. Was that not what she had been banging on about ever since his promotion several years earlier? Still, everything was going to plan. Soon he could retire if he wanted to, and money wouldn't matter. How would he occupy his days then? Gilbert then realised he didn't have a backup plan and dismissed the idea. 'I'll figure something out when the time comes,' he thought.

Feeling optimistic for the first time since Lucy's accident, Holly and Gilbert visited her bedside. When she wasn't napping Lucy would gravely survey her surroundings with her bright blue eyes. She didn't say much, and she couldn't recall her accident. Nonetheless she understood what had happened, and Holly did her best to explain everything. When Lucy's grandmother had passed away a couple of years earlier, Holly learned it was best to furnish Lucy with the facts. Avoiding their unpleasantness was not necessary. Like her father, Lucy preferred to know what was what.

On Sunday morning, just before Gilbert was due to leave for the airport, Lucy asked for a mirror. Reluctantly, he held it in front of her.

Examining every cut, bruise and scar, she simply stated, 'My hair is gone.' She looked at Gilbert with a hopeful smile. 'But it will grow back, won't it, Daddy?'

Gilbert's heart ached. 'Of course it will, my darling, of course it will. You're my beautiful little girl.' Kissing Lucy's forehead, he whispered, 'Daddy has to go and catch a taxi to the airport for work.'

'But wait for Mummy! She's outside at the moment; she'll be back soon.' Lucy was suddenly anxious.

Glancing at his wristwatch, Gilbert found himself wishing he wasn't always in such a rush to be somewhere.

'Okay.' He sighed and tapped the linoleum floor with his foot. He knew his wife had started smoking again and wasn't best pleased about it. But, given the circumstances he had decided not to raise the subject, at least for the time being.

Holly breezed in smelling of roses and cigarettes. Lucy and Gilbert gazed expectantly at her.

'What is it?' Holly asked, curious as to why they were both staring.

'Say goodbye to Daddy,' Lucy said. 'I don't want him to go without saying it.'

'That would never happen, darling.' Gilbert stroked Lucy's pale cheek. For Lucy's benefit he gave his wife an extravagant farewell hug.

'Take care of Lucy,' he whispered, not wanting to leave. Turning to kiss his daughter goodbye, he left the ward.

DONALD WATCHED AS the security office door swung open and Holly stepped through.

'Hello,' he said drily. 'Here to save someone else's career?'

Holly chuckled. 'Actually no,' she replied. 'I'm here to be nosey. I hope you don't mind me asking, but how is Brantley? I haven't seen him for a few days.'

'That's because he's in Leeds. On special leave.'

'Okay.' Holly momentarily examined her hands. They were scrubbed clean. Weeks away from the easel had erased any errant paint stains. 'Well, I was just wondering, that's all.'

'He's back next week as a matter of fact,' Donald said with a resigned sigh. 'At his usual post. You can say hello to him then, assuming of course you'll still be around.'

With that Holly's face lit up. Brantley's future sounded promising, and for a moment she wondered why it even mattered to her. She supposed it was because she could still remember her desolation when her own mother had passed away, and she felt sorry for him.

'You're a good man, Donald,' she found herself saying.

'Not really, love,' he replied, slightly embarrassed. 'Now if you'll excuse me, I have some phone calls to make.'

'Thank you.'

EARLY MONDAY MORNING, Brantley reappeared at his usual post.

'Morning, ma'am.' He gave Holly a tentative smile.

'Hello, Brantley.' She observed his freshly washed and ironed appearance and his forlorn eyes. 'How are you?'

'I'm okay,' he replied. 'Getting there.' Tracing an outline on the ground with the tip of his shoe, he continued, 'I have a gift for you. From Aunty Tilda.' Fishing in his trouser pocket, he extracted a small parcel and handed it to her.

'She didn't have to.' Holly was surprised.

'Yeah, but she was really touched by what you did.' He met her gaze. 'Thank you,' he said.

'It was nothing,' Holly protested.

'It was something.' He cleared his throat. Rifling again in his pocket, he retrieved a crumpled envelope. 'Could you also pass this on to your dad, please?'

'Sure,' she agreed, tucking it into her handbag.

'I'm sorry for what I did.'

'I know.'

'I won't do it again.' Brantley shifted uncomfortably. 'I mean your dad can safely tie his dog up outside again.'

'Forget it, Brantley. It's in the past,' Holly said with a small smile. 'Thank you.' She gestured to the gift. Then, with a delicate wave she was on her way.

Inside the hospital, Lucy was sound asleep in her bed. Holly tore open the small package from Aunty Tilda. It contained a tiny carved jade owl. She held it up to the light and admired its translucency. It was clearly a special piece. Accompanying the owl was a letter, which read:

Dear Holly (I hope you don't mind me calling you that),

Here is a small gift to say thank you for what you did for my nephew, Brantley. He did a foolish thing and is very sorry. We are also very glad you put in a good word with his boss, which earned him back his job, although not without a warning (fair enough too).

I read this somewhere, it's from an ancient philosopher called Philo, 'Be kind, for everyone you meet is fighting a hard battle.'

Brantley is a good boy and what you did was kind. You didn't have to do it, most people would not.

I hope your good father is well and that Sarge is a happy dog now that he's home again. We took good care of him while he was with us, but I don't think he liked my spicy cooking overmuch.

Love from,
Aunty Tilda

Holly smiled as she read this. She remembered when her mum had passed away two years ago and her dad went missing for twenty-four hours. She figured that if he forgave Brantley then Brantley must be alright. She had always thought her father was a good judge of character.

She would return to Larkspur with Lucy that weekend. Holly was itching to pick up a paintbrush again and flexed her fingers in anticipation. She had a lot of catching up to do. Examining her fingernails, she somewhat unusually decided to treat herself to a manicure. She wondered if Tammy might like to join her.

Presently, Dr Roberts entered the ward to check on the still sleeping Lucy.

'Morning!' He greeted Holly with a smile. He was by now accustomed to her being there first thing every day.

Holly returned his greeting and Dr Roberts observed how Holly seemed less edgy now that Lucy had woken from her coma. Late yesterday afternoon he had discovered something rather interesting about Holly, which he was curious to discuss. One of the nurses had recognised Holly's name and told Dr Roberts that she was a reasonably well-known artist.

'I have a non-medical question for you,' he said.

'Go on,' she said, tucking the jade owl and letter into her handbag.

'I was wondering, are you *the* Holly Tatton?'

'Pardon?' She was caught off guard, but quickly recovered. 'Yes, I suppose I am.' She had always imagined her work to be a bit off the mainstream, but never really thought much about it.

'One of the nurses recognised you.'

Holly laughed. 'Oh, I'm hardly recognisable.'

He asked about what kinds of things she painted and Holly did her best to explain. 'Everyday scenes. Are you interested in art?'

'When I have the time.' He checked Lucy's notes for the umpteenth time. 'She's doing remarkably well. This is her last week with us and then she can go home.'

'Yes,' Holly murmured. 'That will be good.' While she couldn't wait for things to return to normal, she knew she would miss Dr Roberts.

Chapter Thirteen.

'DO YOU LIKE it?' Lucy held up the small painting she had been painstakingly working on over several days. It was a picture of Dr Roberts as an angel, but wearing his medical tunic and with a stethoscope around his neck. She had painted it from her bed at home.

'Beautiful,' Holly affirmed.

'It's Gabriel,' Lucy explained.

'I can tell.'

'Shall I give it to him?'

Holly considered this for a moment. She was sure plenty of families returned to hospital with thank-you gifts and cards for the doctors and nurses.

'I don't see why not.' Holly smiled at her daughter. Lucy's sleeping patterns were returning to normal and her hair was sprouting back.

'Four more weeks of rest and you can get out of bed. And then we'll visit the hospital so you can give Dr Roberts your lovely painting.'

Lucy would need therapy to re-train her weak and wobbly legs to walk. It was difficult for her to have to remain immobile for such a long time. Sleeping helped to relieve the boredom, and her bedroom became a menagerie of amusements—books, painting equipment, crafts, dolls and games.

It tore at Holly's heart to see the frustration on her daughter's face at times. She could see Lucy was doing her best to tolerate her immobility. She cried only once, when she learned that her beloved pony, Chester, had been taken away and sold. It was too much for Lucy to bear.

'Not fair!' Lucy shouted, breaking down in tears. 'At least you could have let me say goodbye!' Devastated, she sobbed into her pillow.

'Daddy found a good home for Chester.' Holly did her best to explain. 'You aren't allowed to ride anymore. Not for a long time, darling.'

She stroked her daughter's forehead soothingly. Perhaps it had been unfair of them to sell Lucy's pony so quickly after the accident. Chester had reared up suddenly and thrown Lucy off for no apparent reason. Michael had seen it happen. Lucy remembered nothing. Gilbert and Holly had decided that Chester had to go.

'You could have let me say goodbye. Chester was mine, and I loved him.' Lucy glared resentfully at her mother.

'I know, darling. I'm sorry.' Holly had tried placating her daughter.

'Where's Daddy? Did you sell him, too?'

Holly's jaw dropped. Before the accident Lucy's sunny personality was unfazed by her father's prolonged absences. In fact, she and Holly sometimes even referred to themselves as Batman and Robin, the indomitable duo.

'Lucy, you know very well Daddy is busy with work.' She spoke sternly.

'Yeah, like always,' Lucy replied crabbily.

'He loves you very much and he'll be home soon.'

Lucy refused to be mollified. In the end she drifted off, her brow furrowed in sleep.

Holly tossed and turned in her bed late into the night. Normally Lucy was a bright, easy-going child, but these days she seemed to be persistently unhappy. This bothered Holly a great deal. She distracted herself by toying with the idea of inviting some of the hospital staff along to her upcoming exhibition. Matt, Donald and Brantley could all come, she decided. Should she invite Aunty Tilda, too? She didn't know her, but from her letter and gift, guessed she was a decent person.

Holly was pleased with the way her new paintings were shaping up. During her time in London she had photographed some interesting scenes and people, which she would later paint. One day, she had bumped into a polite beggar in the West End.

'Please, may I have a pound?' His accent had been deceptively posh.

'You can if I can photograph you.' She'd eyed his craggy face with interest.

'Of course you may.' He had been most obliging.

Holly had snapped some photos. Then she had opened her purse, which contained several £50 notes. She'd searched her pockets, but there were no lesser denominations to be found. She'd sighed and handed him a freshly folded note.

'Will this do?'

'Thank you.' He had grabbed it.

Later that evening, Tammy had lectured her against such charitable acts.

'What are career beggars?' Holly had asked. Tammy had rolled her eyes and explained that these unscrupulous types took advantage of well-meaning suckers who gave them money.

'Oh,' Holly had said thoughtfully. Sometimes she knew she had a lot to learn. Fortunately, Tammy was a fountain of knowledge when it came to such worldly matters.

Holly eventually drifted off to sleep. As always when she was tired and stressed, she dreamed in grey and black.

THREE WEEKS LATER Lucy began walking once more, albeit shakily. From the determined look in her eyes, Holly knew she would be running around again in no time at all.

'Can I go and see Chester, Mummy?'

Holly sighed. 'Why would you want to do that, darling?'

'To check he's happy.'

'He's very happy at his new home. You're the one who was injured, not him.'

Lucy still couldn't remember the accident. Dr Roberts had told Holly it was doubtful Lucy ever would. She changed the subject to something more favourable.

'Would you like to visit Dr Roberts in London?'

'Gabriel! Yes, I would.' Lucy instantly cheered up, as Holly hoped she would.

AS USUAL, GILBERT was busy with work. It had been three weeks since Holly and Lucy had last seen him. Since Lucy's discharge from hospital, Gilbert had been working longer than ever, as if to make up for lost time. Although he either emailed or telephoned Holly every other day, she had all but given up asking when he would return to Larkspur. Gilbert would turn up when he could manage it.

One morning, Holly drove herself and Lucy into London. She had been instructed by Gilbert to make a generous financial donation to the hospital. Holly also planned on giving them a painting, one of an abstract, swirling seascape that she had painted recently.

'Hello, stranger.' Brantley beamed as the pair neared the hospital's main entrance.

Holly introduced him to Lucy, who, with a polite smile, shook his hand. Holly then rummaged in her handbag, and produced three envelopes.

'Invitations to the opening of my art exhibition,' she explained. 'There's one for you and Donald. Oh, and one for your Aunty Tilda. It would be splendid if she came along, too.'

During the entire time they were at the hospital, Lucy gazed adoringly at Dr Roberts. Holly was barely able to get a word in edgewise as doctor and patient chattered away. She had already decided to ask Matt—Dr Roberts, she corrected herself—whether these moods swings of Lucy's were normal, and resolved to do so at the next available opportunity—her exhibition.

Chapter Fourteen.

AT THE SOHO-BASED gallery, patrons and guests milled about with fizzing champagne flutes. The exhibition was shared by four artists and was a rather large event. There was a buzz of excitement in the air. Holly recognised a few familiar faces from the hospital. Brantley was accompanied by a brightly dressed rotund woman, who she assumed was Aunty Tilda. She waved and strolled over to greet them. Aunty Tilda enveloped Holly in a ginger-lily scented hug when they were introduced.

'You're a good woman,' whispered Aunty Tilda into Holly's ear. 'A good artist too.'

'It's nice to meet you.' Holly kissed her plump cheek. 'Thank you for your letter and gift.'

They chatted easily for about ten minutes. Holly found herself drawn to Aunty Tilda. She could have stayed longer, but was pulled away by her agent to be introduced to a potential buyer. Her part of the exhibition had been favourably reviewed in the press so far. Recent events had helped channel Holly's creative energy into the right places.

'Remember Lewis Wagnall?' asked her agent, a chic, no-nonsense woman named Anna, who had a nose for making money.

'Are you serious?' Holly hissed incredulously.

'Trust me, he wants to buy something. Just go and say hello for a minute. Be polite and bury the hatchet.'

Holly reluctantly allowed herself to be steered in his direction. He was accompanied by a short, muscular man with mousey hair. He reminded her of a rodent, fresh from the gutter. Lewis uncoiled his long arm and gave her an appreciative up and down stare. They shook hands. His palms were oily.

'Johnson here is a collector from Whitechapel. He loves your work and would like to buy a couple of pieces.' Lewis gave a conciliatory smile. His teeth reminded her of tent pegs, narrow and spaced. Time had not been kind to him; hard living had taken its toll. The whites of his pale eyes were bloodshot, and his face was puffy.

'Is Lucy recovering well?' he enquired smoothly.

Holly stepped back with a start. As far as she was aware Lucy's accident was not common knowledge.

'Fine,' she replied evenly, shooting a pointed look at Anna. She said a few polite words through gritted teeth and looked for an escape. She caught sight of Matt across the room studying one of her paintings. She excused herself and went over to where he was standing. He was smartly dressed for the occasion. It was the first time she had seen him out of medical attire, other than a couple of occasions when they had grabbed coffee from a café nearby the hospital. Then, he had worn a checked shirt underneath his tunic.

Holly was wearing a coral-coloured, Roland Mouret dress, artfully designed to flatter the feminine form without being overt. A pair of killer heels showed off her shapely calves, and her makeup was subtle. The heady rose fragrance she wore completed her image, and for the first time since Lucy's accident, she felt great.

'Hello, Holly.' Matt smiled when he noticed her there. He had been absorbed in one of her paintings. 'You look lovely.'

'Hello Matt.' She greeted him with a kiss to the cheek. 'I mean, Dr Roberts.'

He laughed. 'Come now, it's Matt to you.' He gestured to her painting. 'I didn't know you were so, well, prolific.'

It was Holly's turn to laugh. 'Yes, when the mood

134

strikes me, I suppose I am rather prolific.' Holly noticed that his blonde hair had been neatly trimmed.

Sipping her champagne, Holly felt herself being stared at. She turned around. From a distance, she saw Lewis gazing intently at them. She shuddered.

'Are you cold?' Matt asked.

No, she wasn't. To extract herself from Lewis Wagnall's line of sight, Holly offered to give Matt a tour of the exhibition.

Once out of Lewis's eyeshot, she began to feel more at ease. Guiding Matt from painting to painting, she did her best to explain them to him, without sounding pretentious.

'How is Lucy doing?' Matt asked.

'Actually, I've been meaning to talk to you about her.' They were in a quiet corner, in front of her painting of the West End beggar.

'Before the accident she was happy and easy going. Now, she seems cross with me all the time.'

Matt considered his reply. 'It takes time to fully recover, you know.' He took a small sip of his champagne. 'She experienced a lot of trauma and will still be feeling the effects on many levels. Try not to worry about it.'

'I know.' Holly sighed. 'In no time she'll be good as new, I'm sure.'

'Ah.' Matt nodded. 'See, it seems that way to you and me. Don't forget, Lucy can't remember her accident, she's been immobile for a long time, her hair is still growing back, and she has to learn to walk again. Plus, of course, she can't ride a horse, not for a long time. She's frustrated and doesn't know how to deal with it properly. So she takes it out on her nearest and dearest.'

'She was never like that before.'

'Be patient and don't take it personally, Holly. She'll come round.'

Holly nodded. What he was saying made sense. They continued their conversation, weaving around the paintings.

Before long, Tammy made her ubiquitously grand entrance. She was dressed for the occasion in a fitted black dress, a vintage Chanel jacket and fierce heels that showed off her long, tanned legs. She was accompanied by an obviously younger boyfriend. Spying Holly, she sashayed over, partner in tow.

'Nice paintings!' she exclaimed, waving her champagne flute flamboyantly in the air and nearly spilling its contents down her date's chest. 'The beggar one is particularly good. It turned out well.' She winked slyly at Holly.

After everybody had been introduced, Holly learned that the young man with Tammy was Ted, a Northerner from Preston. He was also a media owner.

'Dating the enemy nowadays?' Holly whispered to Tammy.

Tammy laughed. 'Dating the doctor?' she said quietly.

'As if! You're incorrigible.' Holly poked her arm with a wry smile.

Tammy's irreverent sense of fun captured Holly's mood. She glanced over at Matt, who smiled at her merriment, oblivious to the girl's exchange. Changing the subject, she asked, 'Would you like me to show you around?'

Tammy and Ted nodded.

Presently, they bumped into Brantley and Aunty Tilda, who joined their group. Periodically, Holly was dragged off by her agent to meet potential buyers and other useful contacts, such as art dealers or gallery owners. She was pleased that Lewis and Johnson were nowhere to be seen. She hoped they had gone home.

'Your best work yet,' said several of the dealers and collectors Anna had introduced her to. They nodded approvingly. Holly was grateful for their praise. Art was a fickle business; the various styles went in and out of fashion quickly.

Toward the end of the evening, Anna informed her that about sixty percent of her work had sold already. 'Well done,' she said to Holly. She patted her on the arm. Her eyes gleamed.

'Thank you, Anna,' Holly replied, putting the earlier incident with Lewis to one side.

Anna knew exactly how to work a room to effect. From what Holly understood, she was selective about who she took on, because she liked to dedicate her time to her clients. 'Your success is my success,' was Anna's favourite motto. Their business relationship functioned a bit like Holly's marriage. Holly focused on what she did best—being creative—and Anna took care of the business side of things.

The exhibition eventually drew to a close, and Holly rejoined her friends. By this time everyone had sipped their way through a few glasses of champagne. Tammy and Matt were deep in conversation. It was strange seeing him in this setting, Holly reflected, rather nice in fact. Matt was relaxed and appeared to be having a good time. Even Brantley had cheered up and was looking rather less mournful than usual.

Holly squeezed his arm. 'I'm glad you could come along and that you brought your Aunty Tilda with you.'

Before Brantley could reply, Tammy made an announcement: 'I have a private club membership. What say the six of us go to Shoreditch for cocktails?'

Everyone agreed and piled into a couple of cabs. Before long, they arrived at the East End venue, which occupied the top three floors of a renovated warehouse and had a roof garden.

As it was a pleasant evening, Tammy led the way to the roof garden and found a comfortable spot that was the right size for their group. Patio heaters were alight, as was the city skyline. Holly spied the Gherkin and the Shard in the distance, glittering like jewels in the night. She found herself seated next to Matt who grinned and scooted over to make some extra room for her on the sofa.

'How did it go?' he asked.

'Great,' Holly said with a smile. Since Lucy's accident,

the only time she was able to completely take her mind off things was when she was painting.

The waiter arrived with a tray of assorted cocktails. Tammy had taken the liberty of ordering Holly's favourite cocktail for her, which was a peach Bellini.

They sipped compatibly, Matt on a whiskey sour. Every now and then Tammy and Aunty Tilda pealed with laughter at something amusing Ted was saying. Aunty Tilda had a hearty and infectious laugh, one that made Holly want to laugh, too. Ted possessed a catching sense of humour that was self-depreciating and pricking at pomposity. Even Brantley was smiling. Holly leaned in to hear what Ted was saying. There was a mischievous grin on his round face as he told a joke:

'A lawyer is standing in a long line at the box office. Suddenly, he feels a pair of hands kneading his shoulders, back, and neck. The lawyer turns around, and says:

"What the hell do you think you're doing?"

"I'm a chiropractor, and I'm just keeping in practice while I'm waiting in line."

"Well I'm a lawyer, but you don't see me screwing the guy in front of me, do you?"'

Everyone roared with laughter, including Brantley and Aunty Tilda.

'I hope you don't know any lawyers,' Holly remarked drily to Matt once the laughter had faded.

'Not for a while.' Matt eyes were crinkling at the corners with mirth. A serious look then crossed his face. 'Actually, my father was a lawyer.'

'Was?'

'He died when I was nine years old. Car accident.'

The alcohol had relaxed them more than usual, and Matt was revealing more about himself than intended.

'Sorry to hear that.' Holly looked sympathetically at him. 'Any siblings?'

'One older sister.'

'Lucky you. I always wanted a sister.'

'She's a vet. Married a Kiwi and lives in New Zealand. Plenty of farm animals out there to take care of. I must go out and visit them one day—when can I find some time, that is.' Matt made a face. 'But I don't ever have quite enough of it.'

Holly nodded.

'And yourself, any brothers or sisters?'

'Only child and spoilt rotten of course.' Holly smiled.

'I did wonder.'

Holly looked at him sharply.

'Sorry, I didn't mean it like that. It's just that you're not what I had expected from when you first arrived at the hospital.'

'Oh?'

Matt searched for the right words. 'I suppose I thought you were a poor little rich girl at first. But you're actually quite...' His sentence trailed off.

Holly thought for a moment. She remembered Lewis Wagnall's article, 'Poor Little Rich Girl and Artist.' She shivered.

'Cold?' Matt offered his coat.

'I'm fine. Thanks anyway.' Holly wanted to ask Matt what he had been going to say. She studied her newly manicured fingernails.

'I'm actually quite what?' Her voice dropped an octave.

Matt paused before answering softly. 'Remarkable.' He gazed at her with a friendly expression on his face. 'You're kinder and more generous that most people I come across.'

Their eyes met. Holly looked away.

'Do you have a girlfriend?' She changed the subject and took a sip of her Bellini.

'Not recently, I'm afraid.' Matt turned the heavy whiskey glass in his hand and smiled ruefully. 'Girlfriends need maintenance. My relationship is with work.'

'I know that feeling.' The words were out of her mouth before she could stop herself.

Matt gazed enquiringly at her, unsure of the meaning.

'Gilbert is always working,' she confessed. 'He's not around that much. I'm used to it though.' Suddenly self-conscious, she added with a bright smile, 'He's a good man. We're happy.'

Matt nodded, not saying anything.

'Sorry about that; too much information. I seem to have some kind of compulsive disclosure disorder at the moment. I blame the peach Bellinis.'

'Me too.' He laughed, the tension broken. The waiter approached, cocktails teetering on a tray. He handed them out to everyone.

'That was my round,' Ted said, lifting his drink with a good-natured grin.

'Cheers!' they all said. They clinked glasses.

Everybody except for Aunty Tilda downed their fair share of cocktails. Nonetheless, she somehow managed to be the life and soul of the party.

As it turned out, she had been a model back in her heyday. It was funny, she said, with her skin colour, she was viewed almost as an exotic species. By her account, back then London was not fuelled entirely by sex, drugs and shoulder pads. It was a time of social and economic change, full of movers and shakers. She had appeared in fashion magazines and rubbed shoulders with celebrities. She'd dated photographers and travelled the world. Everyone was absorbed by her fascinating recollections—and there were many. By the end of the evening, everyone was rather worse for wear.

Holly nudged Tammy. 'Ted seems nice,' she said, trying not to slur her words.

'My cougar experiment is going well.' She winked mysteriously. Before Holly could press for details, Tammy glanced at her wristwatch.

'Whoa, I'd better bust a move! Work tomorrow.' She crinkled her nose.

Outside on the street, goodbyes were said and promises

were made to catch up again soon. Taxicabs were hailed, and everyone whirred home for the night. Holly and Matt were the last ones waiting.

Matt offered Holly his coat, which she gratefully accepted. A cab approached with its fare light on.

'You grab this,' Matt said. 'I'll get the next one.'

'Goodnight.' He hugged her before she got in. 'Thanks for the invite. I had a great night. And try not to worry about Lucy.' He kissed her cheek. A flash of light flared suddenly in Holly's peripheral vision. She glanced upwards. Probably just a storm brewing, she thought. She went to hop into the cab.

'Wait!' Matt handed her a slip of paper. 'This is my number, text me when you arrive home safely.' He removed his mobile phone from his shirt pocket. 'Perhaps you'd better give me your number too.'

Inside the cab, Holly basked in the warm glow of success as she entered Matt's number into her contacts list.

She noticed there were numerous missed calls from Gilbert. Dialling into her voicemail, she made out a garbled message, but the reception was so poor that she could only make out a few words, including *Fiona* and *Dubai*.

She glanced at her wristwatch. Should she call him back? She reckoned it would be about 8 p.m. in America at the moment. Dialling Gilbert's number, she heard a beeping sound. Her battery died. She would have to call him back in the morning. The day's excitement and the fuzzy feeling from overindulging had made her eyelids heavy. Her body sank into the warm leather of the taxi seat and she kicked off her shoes. Her eyes closed.

'Miss! You're here.'

Holly's sleepy eyes adjusted to the street lights and she recognised the entrance to Gilbert's apartment building. She peeled herself from the warm back seat and paid the taxi driver, who briefly paused to see her safely enter the building. She stood on the cobbled street, her feet sore from being back in their shoes. She wobbled a little. Gosh, how much did she have to drink? Holly fumbled momentarily with the keypad code to get into the building. She had an uncanny feeling of being watched, but dismissed the thought as drunken paranoia. Once inside, she took the elevator to the top floor. The door pinged open.

Stepping into the marble-tiled hallway she saw a man approach with a cap pulled low to conceal his face. Usually the building was quiet, especially at this hour. Something seemed wrong. At the apartment door she fumbled with the key and quickly stepped inside.

'Hello, Holly.' The man suddenly had his boot in the door. She caught his rank odour of alcohol, cigarettes and sweat. He pulled his cap back and Holly blanched. Lewis Wagnall.

Before she knew what was happening he had pushed his way past her and into the apartment. To Holly's horror, he slammed the door and leaned on it.

'We need to talk.' He slurred, turning the lock. His eyes were glassy and bloodshot.

'How the hell did you get into the building?' She took a few steps backwards.

'Had a bit to drink, did we?' His tone was taunting. 'I followed you from the club. You really should be more careful.'

Holly tried to clear her head and stared at him with as much bravado as she could muster. She wished she were not quite so tipsy. 'Get out.'

Lewis laughed and surveyed the apartment with a sneer. 'Very nice. But money can't protect you forever.'

She sensed something sinister in his tone, but the alcohol had made her woozy and she wanted to throw up. She took a couple of deep, hiccoughy breaths.

'Why are you here?'

He stopped laughing. 'You'd better sit down. You might want to see this.'

'That still doesn't explain what you're doing here.'

Holly moved for the door, hoping to escape, but Lewis was blocking the exit.

'Get out or I'll scream!' She took a breath as if to do so.

Upon hearing her words, Lewis pushed her roughly to the sofa. Her skin crawled at his touch.

'Calm down and listen to me,' he said with some urgency. 'I need to show you something.' Pulling his camera from its case, he turned it on with a beep. 'Here, take a look at this.'

Holly focussed, aghast, at the small camera screen. It was a photo of her and Matt, embracing, snapped as they were leaving the club. From the angle it was taken, it looked as if they were about to engage in a passionate kiss.

'It's not what it seems!' she exclaimed.

'Really?' Lewis gave a twisted smile, his pale pitiless eyes glittering in the half-light. 'What happened then? And why are you still wearing that man's coat?' He plucked at her sleeve. 'He's not your lover, is he?'

'My friend offered it to me, as any gentleman would when a lady is cold. What's it to you anyway?'

His tone was insinuating. 'What would darling Gilbert do if he saw this? In fact, what would you do not to have this little photo here published in the papers?'

Holly moved away and he laughed, following her, making her feel trapped and intimidated.

'Money can't cover up photographic proof now, can it?' He began insulting her, and his words began to spin.

For a split second Holly considered her options. She lunged for the camera, snatching it from Lewis's hands. Dashing to the balcony, she threw the sliding doors open and tossed it over the edge. Somewhere far below, she heard it smash against the cobbles.

She turned around and for the briefest moment, the pair were frozen to the spot like duelling animals. Then, like lightening, Lewis lunged, his face twisted in rage.

'You stupid rich bitch! That was expensive!' Folding his hand into a fist, he slammed it against Holly's face. Her head snapped back against the glass sliding doors of the balcony. The pain was unbearable. She crumpled to the concrete. Lewis was shouting, his spit showering her, but Holly couldn't make sense of the words. Then she was being pulled upwards, but her legs wouldn't move. Her shoes slid off and her backside scraped along the floor. The cold concrete of the balcony changed to the thick pile of luxury carpet. Holly groaned and rolled over. She wanted to lay there, her face buried in the soft comfort. But Lewis had her by the hair and was hissing in her ear. Holly almost gagged on his foul breath.

'I'm the one who put you on the map.' He yanked her hair, hard. 'You should have thanked me. Instead you and your stupid husband made me look like a fool.'

Dragging her to the sofa, he forced her down on the Turkish throw, which felt rough and horrible beneath her skin. One of Lewis's hands pressed against her mouth. The other hand was roughly forcing its way up her beautiful dress and tearing at her knickers.

Holly somehow found the strength to struggle, sheer panic making her eyes wide. She tried screaming, but his hand was covering her mouth. Her teeth found the fleshy part of his palm.

'Bitch!' he snarled, yanking his hand away and stuffing her panties into her mouth. 'You'll pay for that.'

Holly spat them out and thrashed wildly. Opening her mouth, she tried screaming, but no sound came out.

'Have it your way then.' He punched her hard in the face, twice. Blood ran down her chin. Terror thudded dully in her head.

He punched her again. 'This is what you get for being an ungrateful bitch.'

She passed out.

Chapter Fifteen.

HOLLY AWOKE WITH a sharp intake of breath. What had just happened? Her face and body ached. She was in general disarray and her once-beautiful coral dress was torn beyond repair.

With sickening clarity she began to recall events. Her knickers were gone, nowhere to be found. Shifting slightly, she winced with pain. Hoisting herself from the sofa she retrieved her phone from her handbag and plugged it into a power socket.

Staggering to the bathroom, she caught sight of herself in the mirror. A bloodied and bruised face gazed back, something from a horror movie. With shaking hands she wet a washcloth and did her best to clean herself up.

After what seemed like ages she staggered back to her phone, which by now had a small amount of charge on it. There was a text and missed call from Matt, who wanted to know if she had arrived home safely. With shaking hands, she called him back.

'Holly?' His voice was groggy with sleep.

'Something's happened, Matt.' She made a concerted effort to control her breathing.

'Are you okay, Holly? Where are you?' He was wide awake now.

'I was—assaulted.' Holly couldn't bring herself to provide further details beyond that. She almost felt as if she were floating, in a sickening kind of way.

'By who? Where are you?'

'I'm at Gilbert's apartment.'

'Where's Gilbert? Are you okay?'

'Not here. He's away with work.' She fought to regain her composure with more deep breaths. 'Something bad has happened.' The room was spinning so she sat down.

'I'm on my way over now.' His voice was filled with concern. 'Give me about half an hour. What's the address?'

While she waited, she listened to the voicemail Gilbert had left earlier. His sister Fiona needed to borrow the apartment for a few weeks. She had decided to come home when an accountancy contract in Dubai ended. Holly got to her feet. In slow motion she checked the bedrooms. In the master room she saw an inert form on the bed. As her eyes adjusted to the dark she made out a glint of yellow where Fiona's head lay on the pillow. Earplugs. Fiona was also wearing an eye-mask to block out any surplus light. Holly clung to the doorknob to stop herself from keeling over. Fiona had slept through the entire attack.

Closing the door, she stumbled to the nearest bathroom and vomited. After a few moments of heaving she cleaned herself up. Numbly, she located a pair of old flip flops, Gilbert's boxer shorts and an old cricket vest, which she pulled over her tattered dress. Her overnight bag was where she had left it—in the wardrobe of the room where Fiona was asleep. Going in incurred the risk of waking her up. Holly wanted to scream in frustration. With shaking hands she retrieved her badly scuffed shoes from the balcony and stuffed them into her handbag. Then she waited.

WHEN MATT SAW her he was horrified.

'What exactly happened?' He eyed her cut and bruised face with great concern. She was dressed in a weird concoction of Gilbert's clothing and Matt's jacket for warmth. She was shivering.

'Take me away from here and I'll tell you.' She croaked. Matt saw her wide, fearful eyes, even though one of them was badly swollen.

He helped Holly downstairs to where his car was parked on the street, and drove carefully to his Covent Garden apartment.

Once inside, he tended to Holly's facial injuries, applying butterfly stitches in a couple of places. Occasionally she winced in pain.

'Holly,' he said softly, gently wiping the blood from her hair. 'Whatever happened, you're safe now. And when you're ready, you can tell me what's going on.'

Holly nodded. 'Can I have a shower?' She felt dirty.

'Of course. Just try and keep your face dry.' Matt retrieved some clean towels and showed her to the spare bathroom, which was dotted with little flower-shaped soaps. He thumbed through a magazine in the lounge while she showered. After some considerable time, Holly emerged wrapped in a towel, smelling strongly of soap.

'Would it be alright to borrow a bathrobe or something?' she asked. All she had were the clothes on her back and her handbag's contents, including her cell phone and charger.

'My grandmother actually owns this apartment, but she lives with my mother in France. Sometimes she visits for a few days and I take her to the theatre. She keeps a bathrobe here. You can borrow it if you like.'

Holly gratefully accepted the pale pink and fluffy garment, which encased her aching body in soft cotton wool. Then Matt gave her a mug of sugary tea. They sat silently for a while. He watched her anxiously, and waited for her to talk.

Without any inflection Holly finally offered an explanation. 'Lewis Wagnall raped me,' was all she said. She knew he had; the signs were obvious.

'That monster!' Matt's grey eyes flashed with genuine anger. He wanted to badly injure this person, whoever he was, for what he had done to Holly. He liked her a great deal and considered her a friend.

'Who is this Lewis Wagnall?'

Holly did her best to explain. 'An old, sort of…media contact. A creep.'

'You should report him to the police.'

'Don't you have work to go to?' She was stalling.

'I'll call in.' Before she could say anything he grabbed the handset and strode off to the other room. Holly could hear his muted voice through the wall. Presently, he reappeared and sat down heavily. 'I told them I had a family emergency.'

'You didn't have to do that.'

'I hope you don't mind,' Matt replied. 'It seemed like the most, well, discreet explanation.'

Glancing at the mantel clock, he said, 'It might be worth getting a few hours' sleep, then we'll report this to the police. You must be exhausted.'

Holly nodded. Right now she wished she could fall sleep and never wake up.

'Gran likes lavender scented sheets, I hope you do too.' Matt attempted a smile. 'She's originally from Provence and it reminds her of home, I suppose.'

Holly tried to smile back, but instead winced where her lip was cut.

He showed her to the spare room, where, despite her exhaustion, she lay awake for an hour or so, struggling to comprehend her situation. Was it her fault this had happened? Should she have been drunk? She was terrified of what Gilbert would think. She supposed that she was now damaged goods.

Several hours later, Holly awoke with a jolt. It took a moment to figure out where she was and what had happened. Her head and body ached. Getting up slowly, she inched the bedroom door open. There was a carrier bag outside in the hallway, containing some women's clothing, clearly Matt's gran's. There was a note, which read:

These are for you in case you need them. Back in half an hour. Gone to get some supplies. Help yourself to anything you need. M

Holly inspected the bag's contents. She pulled on a thick black jersey dress with a white lace trim, and wrapped herself in a lavender cardigan. She left the belt off the dress; she preferred it baggy and liked the fact it was a size too big for her. As she was pulling on some soft white socks she heard a key in the lock. Holly froze and gripped the sideboard. Matt stepped through the door and saw her there. She was trembling, and felt foolish.

'Are you okay?'

Holly nodded and followed him to the kitchen where he started making some toast.

'Want some?' he offered.

Holly shook her head.

'Would you like to call anyone—Gilbert? Tammy?'

'I'll call Tammy later.'

'Are you sure you don't want to call Gilbert?'

Holly shook her head emphatically. 'I've been thinking,' she ventured. 'Maybe we should call off going to the police.'

Matt stopped buttering his toast. He put down the knife and looked at her.

'This can't be easy for you, Holly. In fact, that's probably the understatement of the year. But if you don't report this, he'll do it again. Do you really want that creep roaming the streets, doing God-knows-what?'

Holly shook her head miserably. 'What if it's my fault this has happened?' she croaked. 'I should have been more careful.'

'It's not your fault, Holly,' Matt said gently. 'You shouldn't blame yourself. You've done nothing wrong. He's the guilty one, not you. You mustn't forget that.'

'I know.' If she sounded unconvinced, it was because she was. 'I'm just worried about what people, what Gilbert...' She trailed off. 'What will people think of me?'

'Your friends and family will support you,' Matt replied stoutly. 'They love you.'

AT THE POLICE station Holly reluctantly gave a detailed statement. They photographed her injuries and examined her for forensic evidence.

Reliving the ordeal was humiliating. Holly gritted her teeth and refused to cry. It was as though she was watching herself as a bystander. Somehow, it didn't feel quite real. She gave them the torn dress she had been wearing when Lewis raped her. Then, at long last, the police were satisfied they had gathered all of the evidence they needed. Before she left they said they would be in touch soon and gave her a telephone number with which to arrange a counsellor. A female officer was put in charge of the investigation and Holly was given her contact details. She was glad she would be dealing with a woman, and not a man.

Matt drove Holly back to his apartment.

'You were very brave,' he said along the way. 'You should be proud of yourself.'

Holly nodded silently. She didn't feel brave at all. Frankly, she would rather forget about it altogether.

'Cup of tea?' Matt asked, once they were indoors.

'Okay.'

They sipped their scalding tea at the dining table. Presently, Matt spoke. 'People will be wondering where you are. Now might be a good time to contact your husband.'

Holly looked into her cup. This was the moment she was dreading most of all.

'Would you like me to call him for you?' Matt offered helpfully.

'Let me think about it.' Holly fetched her cell phone and switched it on. There were several missed calls and an effusive voicemail from her agent, plus some missed calls and a text from Tammy.

Where are you? Saw Lewis outside club! Tried calling, no answer. Call me back. xxx

There was also a text from Gilbert.

Did you get my message about Fiona? Btw, when was exhibition again? Let me know. Work coming out my ears right now. Love Gilbert.

Holly felt empty when she read his message. Gilbert was so very out of touch with her life. She had already told him when her exhibition was, but he must have forgotten.

Her call to Tammy was answered after just one ring.

'Where are you, Holly? I've been trying to get hold of you. I saw Lewis Wagnall near the club last night when I was leaving in the taxi. I tried to call and let you know, but your phone hasn't been on all this time.'

Holly told her where she was and what had happened, at first apprehensively and then engulfed in tears. Tammy listened in silent rage.

Then, carefully, she said, 'You did the right thing going to the police. I'm coming straight over after work. Can I have Matt's address?'

Later that evening, lying on the lavender scented bedspread in Matt's spare bedroom, Holly wept quietly in the arms of her best friend.

Presently Tammy asked, 'Does Gilbert know?'

Holly looked up miserably and shook her head. She could only imagine how ghastly she must look with her bruised face, cut lip and swollen eye.

'He didn't even know the exhibition was on last night.' There was a new bitterness to her tone. She blamed him; he'd said he would 'sort' Lewis out all that time ago. In fact, he was always working, didn't go to any of her exhibitions and seemed more concerned with earning money than spending time with his family.

'Would you like me to call him for you?' It was clear that Holly was reluctant to talk to her husband. 'You need to tell him.'

At last, Holly nodded assent and handed her cell phone

to Tammy. 'It's ringing.' She left the room and closed the door behind her.

After a few tense moments, Tammy reported back that Gilbert would be catching the next plane home.

'How did he seem when you told him?' Holly enquired anxiously.

'Shocked. Furious. Worried. He wanted to speak with you.'

Holly shook her head. 'I'll see him when he gets here.'

A DAY LATER Gilbert was rapping on Matt's front door. They shook hands.

'Is she here?' Gilbert enquired.

Holly could hear his voice from the lounge where she was watching a tacky daytime television show, something she normally avoided doing. Iris sometimes watched them while she was doing the ironing back at Larkspur, but Holly generally tuned out if she happened to be around.

Gilbert stepped into the lounge. Matt was not far behind. Holly looked up. She stayed seated in front of the television. When their eyes met, Gilbert paled.

'Hi,' was all she could muster. She felt as if she were in trouble, and she was also a little cold, but not physically so.

'I'll leave you to it then,' Matt said. 'I'm going out— back in a couple of hours.' He gave Holly an encouraging smile and nod, and then closed the door softly.

Gilbert sat down, studying her with concern.

'Where's Lucy?'

'At Dad's for a few days. She's safe.'

'Are you okay?'

Holly shrugged impassively. 'I suppose so.'

'I'm sorry.' His eyes hinted at a pain more difficult to express.

'It's not your fault. Pity you weren't at the exhibition, but never mind.'

'I was working.' Gilbert was defensive.

'As usual.'

'I resigned.' His voice was quiet.

'Good for you. Fiona was there.'

'Where?'

Holly explained that Fiona had slept through the entire attack at the apartment.

Gilbert blanched. 'It wasn't her fault,' he said eventually. 'I'm so sorry, Holly.' He wanted to reach out to his wife, but couldn't bring himself to do it. Somehow he felt like less of a man. Helpless rage at Lewis Wagnall boiled in his gut. He struggled to stop his mind from wandering into thoughts of revenge.

'Why are you staying here?'

'Tammy shares a house with two other girls. I'm safe with Matt.'

'I didn't know you and Dr Roberts were so…friendly.'

'Matt.' Holly corrected him. 'His name is Matt.'

'I see.'

'There's plenty you don't know about me.' Holly narrowed her eyes.

'That's going to change.' Gilbert spread his hands on his knees.

Suddenly Holly felt something snap inside her. Before she could stop herself, she erupted.

'Well it's a bit bloody late now! If you'd been at my exhibition none of this would have happened! In fact, have you ever been to one of my exhibitions?' She didn't wait for his reply. 'All you care about is money. Why didn't you just adopt a child and hire a nanny? That's pretty much what I feel like most of the time. But do you hear me complaining? No! I get on with it and I'm there for you whenever you need me. Well I'm tired of it. It's one way traffic and I'm tired of it!'

By now she was shouting, her fists balled into small hard fists on her lap. All of her built up anger was unloaded on Gilbert, who sat, listening, looking uncharacteristically small and helpless.

'I resigned,' he repeated, not knowing what else to say.

He thought he had been doing the right thing by working hard to provide for his girls.

Holly stared at him.

'I resigned,' he said again.

She was still glaring at him. 'Why?'

'I had to, they wouldn't let me take time off. I thought about it during the flight back here and I realised that being with you and Lucy is what's important. I did some sums and things; we'll be okay while I figure out what to do next.'

'For once you put me and Lucy first.' Holly's tone was one of surprise. She rocked gently in her seat, her fury waning.

Gilbert swallowed his response.

'Have you been to the police?' he asked eventually.

'Yes.'

'Thank goodness.' His tone became venomous. 'They'd better catch that bastard.' He paused before his next question.

'Are you and Dr Roberts...very friendly?'

'We're not having an affair if that's what you're implying.' Holly stopped rocking.

Despite himself, Gilbert heaved a sigh of relief.

'So what happened exactly...you know...with Lewis?' Tammy had given Gilbert the headline information only.

Holly explained the extra details to Gilbert in a detached kind of way. He asked a few more clarifying questions and she did her best to answer them. He swore furiously when he heard all of what had happened.

'I'm going to kill that sick bastard.' His eyes were icy. He knotted his fists. 'I'll take you home now, to Larkspur.'

'No,' she croaked. Her heart beat faster and her palms were clammy. 'I'm not coming home, not for a while yet. I need some time to think.' She had so much to digest—for instance, if she had not been attacked would Gilbert have resigned? And why only now did he decide that he wanted to be with her and Lucy? One thing was for certain, she did not want to be around him at the moment.

'Don't be silly,' Gilbert said briskly. 'Let's go. You'll have plenty of time for thinking at Larkspur. Besides, you can't stay here forever.'

For a second, Holly wavered. He was right; she must be a burden on Matt.

'You belong at home,' Gilbert continued. 'With me and Lucy.'

'Not at the moment.' Holly stared at her lap.

On it went until Gilbert was forced to accept that no matter what he said, he couldn't persuade Holly to change her mind and return home with him.

'Very well then,' he conceded reluctantly. 'On one condition—promise me you'll stay safe.'

Holly studied her hands and said nothing.

'Promise me,' he repeated hoarsely. 'Please.'

'I always try my best,' she replied.

Gilbert felt sick and afraid. This pale shadow of a woman was a stranger to him.

HOLLY REMAINED TIGHT-LIPPED about Gilbert's visit and Matt didn't press for details. He knew she needed time and space and at least she was safe with him for the time being. But she needed fresh clothing and feminine supplies, that much he knew. He broached the subject after a few days.

'We should really get you some proper clothes,' Matt said, eyeing his gran's black dress.

'No thanks,' Holly replied as brightly as possible. 'This dress is fine. I like it.' The dress hid her curves and was most unflattering. In other words, Holly felt safe in it.

Matt considered his reply. 'Tell you what, let's go for a quick shopping expedition, get you a few basics. I'll come with you.' It had not escaped his notice that she was washing Gilbert's boxer shorts and drying them on the heated towel-rail overnight.

'Alright then,' Holly agreed tentatively. She needed some essentials—new underwear for starters. She liked the safety of Matt's apartment, which was a curious blend of old furnishings and modern appliances. Her confidence was gone and she actually liked Matt taking care of her. It seemed he had become her guardian angel as well as Lucy's. For a moment she was overcome with gratitude, which was quickly replaced by an increasingly familiar hollow and anxious feeling.

'The police phoned.' Matt changed the subject.

Holly felt her heart miss a beat.

'They left a message on the answering machine. Did you get it?'

'What did they say?'

'They found bits of a smashed camera outside the apartment and wanted you to call them back. They think it could be from Lewis Wagnall.'

With shaking hands, Holly dialled the number she had been given for the policewoman in charge of her case. As it turned out they had been to Lewis's apartment and had interviewed him. While they were there one of the officers had spotted a pair of women's knickers, quite torn, stuffed between the cushions of his sofa, and had taken them as possible evidence. They wanted Holly to identify them. If they were hers, they would be tested for a DNA match.

Holly simultaneously felt hope and dread. Hope that Lewis Wagnall would be caught and locked away, ideally forever. Dread because this was not a bad dream from which she could wake up and escape.

Holly retreated to Matt's gran's bedroom. She brooded about Gilbert, whom she held partially responsible. If he had been with her on the night of her exhibition none of this would have happened. In fact, he hadn't attended a single one of them. Not one. She rifled in her handbag for her cell phone and briefly contemplated calling and giving him another piece of her mind. What would she say exactly? Then her eyes fell on the counsellor's telephone number, which had been given to her by the police.

Holly longed to unburden herself on someone who might understand how she felt right now. But in whom could she trust? She was sure counselling services were useful and yet she felt quite uninclined to bare her heart and soul to a complete stranger. Of course she could talk to Tammy, but Holly didn't want her problems to become tiresome. As for Matt, well, she was sure she must be enough of a burden already. It was good of him to put her up like this. She didn't want to hurt her family with the details. She would rather they never found out. She wondered how Lucy was doing, and a dull ache thudded in her chest.

Why me? She constantly wondered. Was this her fault? And then there was the big question: What next? Holly contemplated her future, which seemed very bleak.

She found herself praying, something Gloria said had always helped her. 'God, please give me someone to talk to, someone who'll understand me. Someone I can trust. Someone who won't judge me.'

She heard Matt's phone trill and his muffled voice coming from the lounge. She tiptoed from the room.

'She's okay, Gilbert,' Matt was saying. 'Very fragile at the moment. I'm sure she'll come around. Try not to worry.' He stopped and listened to something Gilbert was saying.

'Yes, I'll keep you posted, don't worry.' He caught sight of Holly and smiled. 'Bye,' he hung up.

Holly stared at him. 'What did Gilbert want?'

'He made me promise to keep an eye on you until you decide what your next move is. I thought I was already doing that. You can't blame your husband for being worried.'

Holly sighed and looked at the carpet. 'Sorry,' she said in a small voice. 'I must be a burden on you.'

'You mustn't think that.' Matt swiftly reassured her. 'You're welcome to stay here for as long as needed.'

Holly looked unconvinced.

'The police found some evidence.' She changed the subject. 'My knickers.' She blushed. 'They've asked me to go to the station and identify them.'

Matt nodded. 'I'll run you there and afterwards we could go for that shopping expedition we talked about earlier. Sound okay?'

They set off for the police station where Holly positively identified her knickers. The police seemed hopeful that an arrest would soon be made.

Afterwards, at a nearby department store, she bought a few essential items. It was the fastest shopping trip of her life. Normally she liked to linger a little. This time, however, she snatched what she needed, paid and left. The crowds made her uncomfortable. Worse still, what if she ran into Lewis?

Matt quietly observed all of this and contemplated gently suggesting to Holly that it might be worth phoning a counsellor. He hoped she would listen to his advice.

Driving back to his apartment, he explained to Holly that tomorrow he needed to return to work at the hospital, and that he was a little worried about leaving her alone.

At the mention of the hospital, Holly thought of Brantley, and then Aunty Tilda.

To Matt's surprise, Holly's face lit up.

'Aunty Tilda,' she breathed. 'Do you think you could get her phone number from Brantley? I think,' she paused before continuing, 'I think I might like to pay her a visit.'

Chapter Sixteen.

'I'M COMING WITH you to Leeds. I have some things I need to do there,' Tammy announced.

'Such as?' Holly looked curious.

'Oh, you know—things.'

Tammy eyed the shapeless, black dress Holly had on.

'Would you like to borrow some of my clothes?'

'No thanks.'

'Doesn't that thing have a belt?' She eyed its empty belt loops.

Holly shook her head with finality. 'This dress is fine.'

Tammy pursed her glossy red lips. Matt's gran's dress had obviously become some kind of safety blanket for Holly. She had even privately broached the subject with Matt, who had sighed and said that he had tried to encourage her to wear something else, but there was nothing much he could do about it for the time being. Considering what her friend was going through, and only for that reason, she made no further comment.

It was a Friday night, and Tammy was staying over. Matt had nipped out to meet a couple of his mates for drinks that evening. With a veritable swag of nail polish bottles in tow, Tammy deftly set about manicuring all available digits. She chose a dark, metallic red for herself, while Holly opted for a pale, inoffensive lilac. Afterwards they would settle in front of Matt's large television and watch an old Audrey Hepburn movie, at Holly's request.

Like Matt, Tammy hoped the police were close to

arresting Lewis Wagnall. Meanwhile, she had decided she would be there for her friend, even if it meant watching movies she had seen before on a Friday night, when partying would have been preferable. She knew where her priorities lay, and she was worried about Holly.

The day before, Gilbert had phoned Tammy for advice, and she felt obliged to give him a few home-truths. He took it valiantly on the chin. He then told Tammy that he had quit his job.

'Well, well, well,' she had marvelled. 'You do mean business after all.'

'Could you talk to Holly for me?'

'And say what, exactly?'

'Just tell her to come home and we'll work this out.' His voice had cracked. 'I love Holly just as much as always, nothing has changed the way I feel.'

Tammy was silent for a minute. 'Okay,' she agreed. 'I'll talk to her.'

Gilbert thanked her.

'Just don't get your hopes up.'

AUNTY TILDA WAS only too happy for Tammy to accompany Holly. If they were driving to Leeds from London then they might as well stay overnight, she said. Aunty Tilda was a natural hostess who relished the opportunity for all kinds of social visits and this was no exception. She had thoroughly enjoyed her night out with the group on the night of Holly's art exhibition. It had made her feel young once more, and she was also mighty pleased to see her nephew, Brantley, smiling again, even if it was just a little bit.

Holly and Tammy set off for Leeds, stopping along the way at a motorway service area for a rare lunch of greasy fries and a burger each. Normally the girls were health conscious, but they had an unwritten rule that when travelling normal diet rules didn't apply.

During the journey, Tammy took back the roof of her

convertible sports car, allowing the sun to find their faces. By now, Holly's face had healed, bar a few shadows and a small, pink scar on her lip—all of which could be concealed with make-up, which Tammy had seen to. Holly turned up the stereo volume and for a few blissful moments she forgot her problems. Closing her eyes she leaned back in the seat, letting the wind blow through her hair. Then her mind drifted to Gilbert. Tammy had passed on the message he had called and wanted her to know that he loved her. As Tammy did this, Holly felt as though a small pick axe were thrust into her chest.

'Too little, too late,' she reminded herself bitterly.

She missed Lucy dreadfully. It had already been three weeks since that fateful night. At least, she supposed, Gilbert was there to run her to and from school and her all-important physiotherapy sessions. She wondered if Gilbert had mentioned anything to her dad. She hoped not. The thought of her family knowing anything about the attack made her deeply uncomfortable.

The unpleasant image of Lewis Wagnall's face drifted into her mind. Holly shuddered and had a hollow feeling, as if something irretrievably important had been snatched from her. No doubt her agent Anna, was wondering where she was. She felt betrayed that Anna had allowed Lewis and his horrid sidekick, Johnson, into her exhibition. Tears welled at the thought of that evening, which had started so well, but had ended up ruining her life, or so it seemed.

Pushing the offending memories from her mind, Holly rubbed her temples as if to try clearing her head. She had a feeling she might be able to talk to Aunty Tilda about all of this. Holly desperately needed to start making some sense of what had happened.

'WHAT'S THAT THING you're wearing?' Aunty Tilda gasped at Holly. A smudge of ketchup was rubbed in to the lace trim of her dress, a leftover from lunch.

Tammy suppressed a giggle, while Holly protectively

smoothed the black granny dress with her lilac-painted fingernails.

'It's very warm. Comfortable, too.'

Aunty Tilda said no more. Instead, she enveloped Holly in a warm, ginger-lily scented hug. She stepped back and surveyed Holly again, almost imperceptibly pressing her lips together and narrowing her eyes. Then she moved on to Tammy and smothered her in a hug, too. She instinctively sensed that things were not altogether right.

'Bring your bags in.' Aunty Tilda invited them inside with a sweep of her dimpled arm. 'Let me show you to your room. You don't mind sharing, do you?'

The girls said they didn't mind and followed Aunty Tilda inside, where the pleasant aroma of cooking spiced the air. Her taste in soft furnishings was rather sparse. Aunty Tilda wasn't a hoarder. In fact, her motto was, 'If it hasn't been used in six months, give it to charity.'

These days Aunty Tilda was headmistress at an inner city primary school. She was a sensible, no-nonsense woman, yet at the same time was caring and a good listener, and she loved looking after people. Because schools so often had to throw things away with each term change she had the same approach to her home. During holidays she volunteered in the local charity shop, primarily so she could chat to people. As a result, the shop often benefitted from Aunty Tilda's generous school donations. Occasionally she even bought extra bric-a-brac home from the shop. She saw it as a form of recycling.

'Here you go.' She led the pair to a decent-sized clean bedroom containing two comfortable-looking single beds. She waddled in and closed the window. 'I'll leave you two to get comfortable. Have you eaten?'

'A while ago,' Tammy replied.

'Good, I'll see you in a bit for a bite to eat.'

'A 'BITE TO eat,' turned out to be rather more than that. By the time the girls made it downstairs, the dining table was laid, and they could hear Aunty Tilda bustling about in the kitchen. She emerged with a slight film of sweat on her still-handsome face. Her perfectly rounded afro was covered with a brightly patterned scarf. When she saw the girls she smiled broadly, her plump cheeks rising to apples. She was looking forward to treating them to some proper Jamaican food. 'These girls need fattening up,' she thought to herself.

She huffed and puffed as she carried the many steaming dishes of food to the table. Holly and Tammy's eyes widened at the curious gourmet arrayed before them. Then Aunty Tilda spooned extra-large portions of rice, peas, chicken, plantain and chips made the traditional spicy way, onto their plates. The girls were too polite to refuse. Besides, it was all rather delicious, and everyone ate more than they should have.

Afterwards, Holly and Tammy insisted on helping with the dishes. When that was done, they made their way into the lounge and settled in the comfortable armchairs there.

'Fancy a drop of ginger rum? It's homemade.' Aunty Tilda smiled indulgently. 'For special occasions.' From a nearby cupboard, she produced a large glass bottle filled with a pale amber liquid and held it up. Her ginger rum was actually quite famous among family and friends for its multiple uses, from a cure for coughs and colds, to a strong, sweet digestif following a large meal.

'Why not?' Holly accepted. She could do with a drink. Tammy followed suit.

Holly gulped hers down immediately, and belched softly. 'Pardon.' She looked slightly embarrassed. 'It's been a long day.'

Tammy stifled a giggle. Aunty Tilda refilled Holly's small glass and looked meaningfully at her.

'There be something on your mind young lady?'

Holly's heart skipped a beat. She paused before answering. 'A few things,' she admitted.

'Mmm-hmm.' Aunty Tilda nodded knowingly. She

wriggled her large behind into the sizable, squishy leather armchair.

'Well, you're at the right place, my dear. I could tell as soon as I saw you that something was up.' She took a dainty sip of ginger rum and smacked her lips together. 'You and I can talk about anything when you're good and ready.' She leaned over and patted Holly's hand. 'You're safe here.'

Holly nervously gulped down another large mouthful of her drink. She sat silently for a few moments and twisted a strand of hair around her forefinger.

'The night of my art exhibition…' She trailed off.

Aunty Tilda nodded encouragingly and Holly took a deep breath.

'That night something terrible happened when I got back to Gilbert's apartment. He wasn't there though. Just his sister was and she was sleeping.' Picking up her glass, she drained what was left in it. By now, Aunty Tilda was watching Holly with some concern.

'Can I have some more?' the rum made Holly feel light headed and it warmed her belly.

Aunty Tilda topped up her glass carefully. Holly took another, large slug.

'I was raped, Aunty Tilda,' she blurted out once the burning liquid had gone down. 'By someone I know.' She looked miserably at her feet. 'There, I've said it. He was at my exhibition that night. I've reported it to the police and hopefully they're going to make an arrest soon.'

'Oh love. Lordy,' Aunty Tilda said with a mixture of horror and consternation. 'Go on.'

'The thing is, Aunty Tilda—are you sure I can call you that?'

Aunty Tilda nodded emphatically. Almost everyone she knew called her that and she liked it that way. At school she was simply known as 'Miss.' All the teachers were. That was how it was.

Holly nodded. 'Well, I feel…wretched. Like I should

have prevented it somehow. Like I'm to blame.' Holly picked savagely at her fingernail. 'And I'm angry with Gilbert—why wasn't he around to protect me?'

Aunty Tilda nodded sagely as she digested this information. Tammy silently sipped at her drink.

'I feel so worthless. Who would want me now?' Holly banged her glass down. 'I'm damaged goods, even Gilbert doesn't want me. He's hardly ever there. He wouldn't touch me when I told him.'

Everything came tumbling out. Holly described the awful events of that night, including the part where Fiona had slept through the entire thing.

'Gilbert's never been to a single one of my exhibitions in all the years I've been an artist. Not one! He says he resigned from his job, but it's too little too late.' Her tone was rancorous. She rubbed her temples. 'Could I please have a little bit more of that?'

'Holly, listen here. It's not your fault,' Aunty Tilda stated, looking pointedly at her, as two fingers of rum sloshed from the bottle and into Holly's glass. 'You remember that. That person Lewis had no right to do that bad thing to you. You did nothing wrong; he's a bad person, not you. And you're brave going to the police. Some people could not do that.'

Holly considered this. 'Maybe you're right,' she replied, somewhat doubtfully.

'I'm right,' Aunty Tilda asserted firmly. 'It's not your fault. He attacked you because he's evil. People like that should be locked up. Forever.'

'It's not your fault, Hol,' Tammy repeated. 'Please stop thinking it is.' She was crying.

A bout of the hiccups suddenly engulfed Holly. Aunty Tilda went to the kitchen to fetch her a glass of water.

They continued talking and drinking late into the night.

Tammy didn't say much. She took everything on board. She, too, was learning.

THE NEXT MORNING, Holly awoke with a dull headache and swollen eyes. Last night had been a watershed and she had cried her eyes dry. Considering the sizeable portion of Aunty Tilda's rum she had tucked away, it could have been worse. She hoped she hadn't said anything too embarrassing.

Pulling on her dress, she wobbled to the bathroom and inspected herself in the mirror.

Large, sad, toffee-brown eyes gazed back. Her face was pale and a sprinkling of freckles stood out on her nose. Suddenly she smiled and her reflection was transformed. She touched her lip where it had healed. Matt had done a good job of patching her up.

Last night had been cathartic. Today for the first time she felt a tiny pinprick of hope. She wondered how Lucy was, and whether she should call her. It had been too long since she had last seen her daughter and she missed her every second of each day.

There was a tap on the door. 'Are you in there, Hol?' Tammy's voice was faint. 'I need to wee. All that rum, you know.'

'All yours,' Holly said, hastily throwing open the door and making a quick exit.

In a few moments, Tammy stepped back into the bedroom. She flopped on the bed. 'Coming shopping today?'

'I don't think so.'

'C'mon, Hol. I really need your opinion on some lipstick colours.'

Holly looked doubtful.

'Go on…'

Holly considered Tammy's offer. Now that she mentioned it, she probably could do to buy a few extra supplies for herself. 'Alright then.'

Tammy bounced gleefully, up and down on her bed. Suddenly she stopped and sniffed the air.

'Mmm,' she said. 'Bacon, perfect for a hangover.'

The girls sloped downstairs and into the kitchen where

Aunty Tilda was clattering about with some cooking utensils. She looked like a bright summer's day in her flowing orange patterned tunic and black leggings. A large pair of purple dome earrings clung to her earlobes. Tammy figured she must be about fifty, but you couldn't really tell. 'Black don't crack,' an ex-boyfriend of hers once said— rather smugly, Tammy had thought at the time. She supposed then that Aunty Tilda was of indeterminable age.

'Morning!' She waved a fish slice at them and looked remarkably cheery. 'Sit down girls; breakfast is about ready.' She gestured to the already laid dining table.

'How are you feeling, wee loves?' She smiled indulgently. She had a handsome face, with wise, dark eyes and a warm smile.

Despite Holly's headache, she found herself smiling back at her. 'I'm okay,' she replied.

Tammy gently nodded in agreement. Moving her head about too much hurt. She always had been a bit of a lightweight; Holly on the other hand drank like a pirate when the mood took her. This was an ongoing source of disappointment for Tammy, because it didn't happen often enough for her liking.

Aunty Tilda liked seeing Holly smiling. Dishing up some crispy bacon rashers and fried eggs, she smacked her lips together.

'You're welcome to stay a few more days, Holly dear; might do you some good to get away from it all,' she said.

'I don't know... I don't have too many spare clothes with me.' Holly didn't want to impose.

'Let's have breakfast and go shopping,' Tammy offered.

'Good idea,' Aunty Tilda said quickly, trying not to look too pointedly at Holly's dress.

After breakfast and some major cosmetic ablutions, Tammy hustled Holly out of the door and into her car.

They drove into the centre of Leeds, to a large and bustling shopping mall. Holly glanced down and noticed for the first time the ketchup stain on her hem.

'I might need a new dress,' she murmured, slightly horrified at her own slovenliness.

'Let's do that first.' Without delay, Tammy propelled Holly into a nearby department store where they found themselves beside a Joules clothing rack. Perfect. Practical, wholesome and stylish—just right for Holly now.

'What do you think of this?' Tammy held up a pretty flower patterned shift dress. It looked as if it might give Holly the cover she craved.

Holly eyed it dubiously. 'Too short.'

Tammy whipped through several more clothing racks.

'How about these?' She produced several sturdy dresses, and held them up.

Holly pointed to the pink and navy jersey tunic, which finished on the knee. 'That one looks alright.' She headed to the changing room with it.

Tammy followed her. 'What about a belt? You know, just nip it in at the waist a bit.' She inspected the frock Holly was trying on.

'Nope, it's fine as it is,' Holly replied, straightening up.

Tammy knew when to give in. It wasn't quite to her taste, but it was a vast improvement on that dress Holly had been wearing for weeks on end, which was by now becoming, well, ripe. She smiled as they strolled from the shop. Holly was wearing the frock she tried on earlier and had with her a couple of other purchases, too. Tammy hoped it might be a small step in the right direction toward Holly's recovery.

'Coffee?'

'Yup,' Holly agreed. It would certainly help stave off the effects of last night. 'Didn't you want to look at some make-up as well?'

Tammy had almost forgotten about that. 'Of course!' she said, almost a bit too cheerfully.

After their coffee Tammy tried on some lipstick. For good measure, she purchased three tubes. She didn't need any of it—the whole shopping trip had been an elaborate ruse to get Holly into some decent clothes, and, more importantly, back to the land of the living.

After dropping Holly off at Aunty Tilda's, Tammy hugged them both and said her goodbyes. She intended to return to Leeds the following weekend and drive Holly back to London. She wasn't sure where to, back to Matt's perhaps. She felt an unexpected pang of sympathy for Gilbert. He and Lucy must be missing Holly a great deal. Still, Holly needed to work through her ordeal in her own time. Aunty Tilda's company certainly seemed the ideal remedy for that.

WHEN TAMMY SAW Holly the following Saturday afternoon she was wearing another new frock. There was a flush of colour in her cheeks and Aunty Tilda's cooking had helped put some meat back on her bones. In fact, she had even taken it upon herself to teach Holly the art of traditional Jamaican cooking. To her satisfaction Holly had proved to be an apt pupil.

'The police got the DNA results back.' Holly looked pleased. 'Lewis was arrested yesterday. Turns out he has a record for attacking women. When he was at university, he assaulted some girls there, but they dropped the charges later.'

'Let's go out for dinner,' Tammy suggested, feeling elated at this piece of news. 'My shout. You're very brave, Holly. If you didn't report this, that monster would still be walking the streets as a hazard to women-kind.'

Suddenly, Holly looked doubtful. 'I don't know. It all still has to go to court.'

'CAN I TAKE your order, ma'am?' A friendly-looking waiter appeared at Aunty Tilda's elbow.

'My usual, thank you.'

Holly and Tammy exchanged looks. Obviously, Aunty Tilda was a regular here.

'Same here.' Holly ordered, trusting Aunty Tilda's lead.

'Me too.' Tammy echoed, guessing she was in for a treat.

With an obliging nod, the waiter scribbled something on his tiny notepad and scurried off to the kitchen.

Tammy drained her wine. 'So,' she said, turning to Holly with a happy smile. 'Where am I taking you tomorrow?'

Holly glanced at Aunty Tilda, who nodded encouragingly.

'Home please,' she replied. 'To Larkspur—if you don't mind giving me a ride.'

Of course Tammy didn't. She leaned over and hugged Holly. 'Don't be silly, it would be my pleasure.'

Chapter Seventeen.

LUCY HAD PRACTISED walking with grim determination. Her efforts quickly began to pay off and in no time at all she was pretty good at moving about, albeit a little shakily. Her weekly physiotherapy visits had also helped regain her strength and coordination. Lucy knew she wouldn't be returning to ballet classes anytime soon, nor, for that matter, horse riding. Her mother had explained all of this to her and it irked Lucy a great deal. She couldn't remember falling from Chester, her normally placid and beloved pony. She was certain that he would never have reared up, unless something had startled him—a fox perhaps? She would never know for sure, which also bothered her. She would wake suddenly at night from a vague dream of falling, which always ended with her hitting the ground with a painful thud. Try as she might Lucy failed to recall a single detail of the accident. The other irksome thing was that her parents had sold Chester without telling her. She missed him a great deal.

Lucy directed much of her pent up anger and frustration in the direction of her mother. In fact, she even got the blame for her dad's prolonged absences. She missed him and, at times, was lonely. Her school friends dropped by from time to time, but it only reminded her of all the fun she was missing out on. Looking in the mirror was unpleasant—the cuts and bruises had faded to horrid pinks and yellows, and her hair was still sprouting back.

She missed her long hair and hated the short, blonde spikes she was left with. Try as she might to snap out of her grim mood, there were many occasions when Lucy was unable to contain her emotions. Sometimes she even said things to her mum that she knew would hurt her. Saying them felt good at the time, but immediately afterwards when she saw the bewildered look in her mum's eyes, she felt worse than before. Then, to top it off, her mum had vanished for weeks on end. Her dad suddenly showed up and was home all the time. He seemed to be saying that he wouldn't be leaving Larkspur anytime soon, and that he had finished with his job.

Lucy was far too down in the dumps to be even slightly pleased about this news. On any other occasion, she would have been beside herself with happiness. Although she didn't say anything, Lucy feared it was her fault that her mum had vanished, and that her bad moods had driven her away for good.

IRIS, THE EVER trusty figure in Lucy's life, did her best to carry on as normal. She, too, worried about recent events. It had all started with a strange and rather disjointed phone call from Holly after her art exhibition, asking her to contact Will to let him know that something had come up, and could Lucy stay on with him for a few extra days? Then Gilbert had suddenly appeared from out of the blue. It was obvious something wasn't right. Nonetheless, Iris knew it wasn't her place to ask too many personal questions.

Some years ago and unbeknown to Gilbert, she and Holly had agreed that Iris would take every Wednesday off work. It allowed Holly the freedom to potter around Larkspur as she wished. If Holly ever needed Iris's help, she was only a phone call away. And so it was that Holly and Iris settled into an agreeable routine, which varied only if Gilbert was about. Now, it seemed Gilbert was home for good.

And so with a pink face, Iris confessed to Gilbert what she and Holly had arranged all that time ago.

To her relief, Gilbert wasn't angry. In fact, he conceded there was nothing that could be done about it. If that was what had been agreed between his wife and Iris, then he would honour it. Besides, he had other, rather more pressing matters to consider, including whether Holly was returning to Larkspur, and what to say to people who asked where she was.

'IS HOLLY THERE?' Will's gruff voice crackled down the telephone line.

'I'm afraid she's not about at the moment. Could I get her to call you back?'

'I've been trying to reach her on mobile for the last couple of days, but she's not answering. Where is she?'

'Well…she's having sort of a mini-break. In Leeds. With the stress of her latest exhibition and Lucy's accident, she decided to get away from it all and stay with a friend for a bit.'

'When is she back?' Will sounded unconvinced.

'Oh, you know. In a few days, or so.'

'Well, please tell her I called.'

Will changed the subject before Gilbert could reply. 'How are you anyway, son?'

'Fine thanks. I've left my job to spend more time with Holly and Lucy. Share the load, you know.'

'Good for you.' Will sounded pleased, if not rather surprised.

'And how are you?'

'Same as always, staying out of mischief. When you see Holly next, tell her to call me back, will you? I've got something I need to tell her.'

Gilbert heard Spock barking and the sound of a car approaching the house. Every day that Holly was gone, he hoped he might see her pulling up to Larkspur in that car of hers.

Saying goodbye and hanging up, Lucy, who was hovering in the background, asked, 'What did Granddad want?'

'To speak with Mummy.'

'When is Mummy coming back?' Lucy asked this same question every single day. It was late morning and Gilbert figured it was better to get it out of the way sooner rather than later.

'She's having a little holiday with a friend.'

'When is she coming home?'

Before Gilbert could reply he spied a red convertible, which was being parked outside the main entrance of the house. It looked like Tammy's car. He sprinted downstairs. Sensing something was afoot, Lucy followed behind him as quickly as she could.

Presently, the doorbell rang. Gilbert was already beside the heavy oak front door.

'Tammy?' he began, swinging the door open.

He gasped when he saw Holly there. Tammy was beside her with a supportive arm around her waist and Spock was wagging his tail enthusiastically and licking Holly's hands in delight.

'Hello, Gilbert.' Holly looked nervous.

'Mummy!' Lucy squealed, throwing herself at her. Her blue eyes shone with joy.

Holly scooped her up and into her arms. She inhaled Lucy's familiar and clean cucumber smell. Tears pricked at her eyelids.

'I was worried about you.' Lucy's voice was muffled by Holly's shoulder. 'I thought maybe you weren't ever coming home.'

'You mustn't think that, darling. I would never leave you—or Daddy.' A lump came to Holly's throat.

She looked up at Gilbert, who stood there with suspiciously shiny eyes.

'Holly, welcome home,' Gilbert hugged them both. He smelled of his usual aftershave and she felt his damp cheek against hers.

She had been dreadfully nervous about returning home. For the first time in her life she was fragile and unsure of her worth as a person and whether she would still be accepted and loved by Gilbert after what had happened. Fortunately her week with Aunty Tilda had gone some way towards allaying her fears. She had been quick to reassure her that what Lewis had done was not Holly's fault and to keep her head high. Otherwise Lewis would succeed in what he had set out to do—punish, dominate and degrade Holly for some years-old grudge he had been nursing against her and Gilbert.

Tammy cleared her throat. 'Well, I'd best be off.' She glanced at her wristwatch. 'I have a few things I need to take care of this afternoon.'

Holly disentangled herself from Lucy and Gilbert. She grasped Tammy's hands.

'Thank you, Tammy.' Her eyes were moist with tears.

'Don't mention it,' she replied, hugging Holly tightly. 'Call me if you need anything.'

They waved goodbye and Spock barked as Tammy's car retreated down the drive. A smile played on Tammy's cupids bow lips as she drove away. It warmed her to see Holly's pleasure at being reunited with her family.

It was not over quite yet, though. The date for Lewis's court appearance was approaching and Holly would be required to give evidence. Tammy knew just how much she was dreading that.

LUCY WAS GLUED to Holly's side for the remainder of the day, which was mostly spent in Larkspur's big kitchen. It tended to be the hub of the house, as kitchens so often were. Holly decided to act as normally as possible and busied herself with making chocolate cupcakes, Lucy's favourite. Thankfully Iris could always be counted on to keep the cupboards well stocked with food and cooking ingredients.

Gilbert hovered in the background, not taking his eyes

off his wife, and dipping into the conversation from time to time. As Lucy chattered about her walking, it occurred to Holly that it might be worth getting Lucy involved with some new, gentler hobbies that didn't involve horses or ballet. Art classes perhaps? Piano? She mentioned this to Lucy, who beamed in return.

'Actually, Mummy, I've been practicing drawing.'

Holly watched Lucy teeter off to retrieve her drawings from her bedroom, leaving Holly and Gilbert on their own for the first time since she had returned home. Lucy's movements had become more fluid since Holly had been away. She smiled as she mixed the cupcake batter. It was just a matter of time before Lucy was back to her good old self.

'Penny for your thoughts?' Gilbert asked.

'I was just thinking how well Lucy is doing.'

'Yes, she is.' Gilbert's tone was gentle. There was a small pause before he added, 'And how are you doing?'

'Don't.' She stopped stirring. 'Not now, I mean.' The smile faded from Holly's face and she began spooning the mixture into paper cups, her head down.

She changed the subject, 'Do you miss your job?'

'No. I'd rather be here, with you.'

Lucy reappeared with her sketch pad in hand. She put it on the marble bench top and opened it.

'Look, Mummy.' Lucy leafed through the pages and described each drawing at length, explaining what they were and why she had drawn them as she had.

They were rather good, Holly thought. She resolved to cast around for art classes on Monday.

THE NEXT DAY, the sky was so blue that when Holly opened the curtains, she could almost taste its freshness. It was a jot before eleven o'clock in the morning. She had slept so deeply that when she awoke, for a moment she didn't know where she was.

She rubbed her eyes. Gilbert was gone from their massive bed. He had not touched her the night before other than to give her a quick peck on the cheek and wish her goodnight. He had offered to sleep in another room, but Holly thought that would not be necessary.

Pulling on her dressing gown, Holly padded downstairs to the kitchen. She could hear muffled voices from behind the closed door. Opening it, her eyes fell on her father and Gloria sitting opposite Lucy and Gilbert at the island in the centre of the large kitchen.

She froze for a second. What was Gloria doing here? Did they know? Her insides clenched and for a second she felt dizzy. She took a deep breath.

'Gloria, Dad, hi.' Her eyes flicked between their faces.

'Hello, darling!' Her dad stood up and hugged her, followed by Gloria.

'My fault,' Gilbert said. 'I forgot to pass on the message that they were dropping by for a visit today. Coffee?'

'Sure, okay.' Holly weakly slid into a chair. 'So how are you both? It's nice to see you here, Gloria.'

Last time Gloria visited Larkspur was when Holly had thrown a birthday party for Lucy. She had needed the extra pair of hands, and the supervision of multiple excited little girls.

Gloria fluffed her curls a little. 'Fine thanks, dear.' She glanced at her father who had obviously twigged that something was up. 'Your father and I have something to tell you.'

'Sure.' Holly's brow furrowed a little, perplexed.

Gilbert placed a steaming mug of coffee on the counter his eyes fixed on Holly as he did so, while Lucy munched thoughtfully on a chocolate cupcake.

'See, the thing is,' Will began. He looked at Gloria, who smiled at him encouragingly.

Holly looked expectant as she reached for the sugar.

'Gloria and I have become quite close.' He put his big paw on Gloria's hand. 'And, um, I've asked her to marry me, and she's accepted.'

Holly's teaspoon clattered to the marble bench top.

'Married?! Wow! Well…congratulations!' Holly took a gulp of coffee and winced when it scalded her oesophagus. 'When did this happen?'

'Well, after your mother passed away…Gloria helped me through a tough time in my life.' Frowning at the recollection, Will cleared his throat and continued. 'We grew quite close, and in the past year or so, well, things became…' He cast about for a suitable word—'Romantic.'

Holly gaped at them, appalled that she hadn't picked up on any of the signals. 'Congratulations,' she repeated, unable to think of anything else to say.

Looking up at Gilbert she saw he was gazing intently at her with a funny expression in his blue-green eyes. Lucy looked down at her plate and continued to chew slowly.

'You both knew?'

'Um, yes, we'd just finished telling them,' Will confessed. 'We wanted to wake you, but Gilbert insisted you needed sleep. Is everything okay? I've been a bit worried about you lately. I haven't been able to get hold of you. You're not, pregnant, are you?' He sounded hopeful.

Lucy looked up, also hopeful. Gilbert suddenly froze.

'No.' Holly almost choked on her coffee. Standing abruptly, she rather clumsily moved to hug them.

'I'm happy for you both.' She smiled brightly. 'Anyway, I'd better get properly dressed. Care to stay for lunch?'

'That would be good,' her dad said.

'I'll rustle something up, shall I?' Gloria looked eager.

'Gloria, you're a guest here, so please just relax. You don't have to do anything.'

Her face dropped and Gilbert, noticing this, stepped in.

'I'll take care of lunch,' he offered. 'Shall we have it in the conservatory?'

'No!' Holly almost shouted. That room reminded her of the interview with Lewis all those years ago.

'Why don't we have it in the dining room instead? It's a special occasion after all,' Gilbert suggested.

Holly nodded and left, practically hyperventilating.

Outside, she sagged against the wall. There had been so many changes, so much to take in and she felt as if she were losing control. It was all just a bit much. A nice scented bath might help clear her head, she decided.

'SO, HOW WAS Leeds?' her dad was buttering a chunk of freshly-baked bread that Gloria had bought along.

In spite of Holly's mental preparation for the inevitable questions, she still felt awkward.

'Fine thanks. Pass the salt please, Lucy darling.'

'Gilbert tells us you were visiting an old friend.' Gloria smiled at her.

'That's right,' Holly replied.

'She needed a break.' Gilbert smoothly chimed in.

Holly nodded. 'So, anyway, I'm back now!' Her tone was determinedly bright. She clapped her hands, 'Tell me all about your, ahem, romance—how did it happen?' She squeezed Gloria's arm. 'I'm so happy for you,' she whispered. It was true, even though she was still getting used to the idea.

Fortunately, no more questions were asked about her trip to Leeds, thanks in no small part to Gilbert, who nimbly deflected them and steered the conversation back around to her father and Gloria's impending marriage.

'Do you have a ring?' Gilbert smiled encouragingly at Gloria, who modestly held out her left hand and waggled her ring-finger. Upon it was a sparkling diamond solitaire in a rub-over setting.

'Pretty but practical,' she stated, looking shyly at Will, who gazed fondly back at her.

'Platinum is a sturdy metal,' he added.

Holly thought it was a lovely ring.

Gloria had practically been a part of their family since Holly was a little girl. She trusted her implicitly and knew her mum would be pleased that her dad had finally rediscovered happiness. Holly smiled at her dad and Gloria. She was genuinely pleased for them.

Chapter Eighteen.

'HOLLY! WHERE HAVE you been?' It was Anna, her agent. 'You seem to have fallen right off the radar lately! Is everything quite alright?'

Holly had been dreading this moment for some time.

'I'm fine.' She paused. 'In fact, I've been meaning to speak with you.'

'Great!' Anna launched into a monologue about sales at Holly's recent exhibition, the compliments from critics on her work, and opportunities for more exhibitions.

Holly listened patiently until at last, Anna stopped.

'Anyway,' she continued. 'As I said, I've been meaning to speak with you.' Her voice dropped an octave.

Something in Holly's tone made Anna stop and listen.

'I no longer need your services as an agent.' Holly was blunt. She had anticipated what to say and concluded that dropping Anna in person was better than doing it over email—as Tammy was want to do with unwanted boyfriends.

'Why?' Anna gasped. She thought all had been well.

'You're a talented agent, Anna, but I've found somebody else who is better suited to my needs.'

From the corner of her eye, Gilbert was giving her the thumbs up. He had been coaching her on what to say.

'What did I do wrong?' Anna's normally brisk tone was uncharacteristically wheedling. The thought of her cash cow slipping away dismayed her.

'You specifically went against my wishes and allowed Lewis Wagnall into my exhibition.'

'But his friend wanted to buy something!'

'And did he?'

She paused before replying. 'No.'

'My lawyers will be in touch tomorrow to tidy things up. I'm sorry.'

There was a stunned silence.

'Who is replacing me?'

'My husband. Goodbye.' With a trembling hand, Holly hung up and looked at Gilbert. He hugged her.

'Well done, darling,' he whispered into her freshly washed hair. 'You did the right thing.'

Holly's eyes searched his face. 'Are you sure you want to do this?'

FOR SOME TIME now, she and Gilbert had been having many heart-to-heart conversations, hoping they could work through what had happened. This proved somewhat difficult, and on several occasions they fought bitterly. Holly confessed that she blamed Gilbert for not being there to protect her from Lewis Wagnall. Gilbert admitted he was struggling with the feeling that their marriage was somehow tainted. He also blamed himself for not being around to protect Holly. Things became so heated that Holly threatened to pack up her things and leave. Their discussions had become circular in nature and were going nowhere fast.

It was at this point that, as a last resort, they called a counsellor. Although it wasn't easy for them to discuss the traumatic event, from their weekly sessions, their perspectives gradually shifted, and they realised Holly's rape was not anyone's fault other than Lewis's, and his fault alone. Blaming themselves and each other for what he had perpetrated was quite simply, ridiculous.

Their counselling sessions helped them to process their painful thoughts and emotions, and, gradually, their natural trust and affection for one another was restored. It was still too early for physical intimacy and both Holly and

Gilbert realised this. It had been a long time, and Gilbert was beginning to plot romantic ways in which he could seduce Holly without scaring her off.

HOLLY WAS WEARING her best and only business suit, reserved for meetings with important art gallery owners. It was formal yet feminine and the double string of pearls twisted around her neck worked well with it.

The court hearing was excruciating. Gilbert sat beside Holly, his jaw clenching and unclenching. Tammy, Aunty Tilda and Matt sat on her other side. In due course Tammy and Matt would be called forward as witnesses, as would Holly.

Eventually it was her turn. She took the stand and gave her evidence as best she could. During the questioning from Lewis's lawyer, her voice wobbled a couple of times, and she had to stop and take some deep breaths to settle down.

Afterwards when she was seated, Gilbert took her hand. It was trembling. Seeing Lewis across the courtroom glowering at her was bad enough. Having to relive the experience in front of the whole courtroom was worse yet.

'How do you plead?' the judge finally asked, looking at Lewis.

Silence. From the corner of her eye, Holly saw Lewis's lawyer prod him with an elbow.

'Guilty.' Lewis looked defiant.

It was obvious that Lewis actually believed himself to be innocent. The only reason he pled guilty was because his lawyer had advised him to do so, in order to hopefully reduce his sentence.

Holly's own lawyer was quietly confident that the case would be over quickly, with only one outcome likely. That was mostly because of the compelling evidence, which held against Lewis's innocence.

'You did the right thing going to the police as soon as possible,' her lawyer, Samantha Howell, had said. She was the best in the business. Gilbert had personally selected her.

Afterwards, when the court session was adjourned until sentencing, Holly hugged each of her supporters, and with each embrace the nervous tension seemed to drain away.

GILBERT'S BAG CLINKED as he strolled into the kitchen late in the afternoon. Holly was preparing a Jamaican dish for dinner. Aunty Tilda would be proud.

'What's that you've got there?' Holly looked up from the onions and chopping board. She wiped her eyes.

'Champers.' Gilbert grinned, carefully placing an expensive looking carrier bag on the bench top. He removed a bottle from the bag and brandished it with a hopeful look in his eyes. 'Fancy a glass?'

It was a Wednesday, which meant Iris had the day off. Lucy was with her new art tutor, a quirky local artist and children's book illustrator named Willow Phillips. Lucy loved her twice weekly sessions after school. Today she was also playing at a friend's house afterwards. Chester had not been mentioned for ages. In fact, as Lucy's hair grew and her injuries faded, her overall mood improved, too. She still couldn't recall the accident, but these days it seemed to bother her increasingly less, and she began to resemble the bright and easy-going little girl of old.

Holly hesitated. She was about to decline, but remembered that Iris and Lucy were not around.

'Sure, why not?' She flashed a small smile at Gilbert.

Wasting no time, Gilbert deftly popped the cork and filled two flutes with the frothy liquid.

Holly sipped at the velvety bubbles, savouring its taste and texture. Since their counselling sessions and Lewis's recent conviction, their relationship seemed to be moving forward. She no longer felt stuck in limbo and sensed that Gilbert was feeling better about everything, too.

They chatted about Holly's next exhibition, which would take place in about six months' time. It was a gamble for

Gilbert to take the role as Holly's agent, but given his never-ending connections, they were sure it would work.

Her next exhibition would be a solo showing at a swanky West End gallery, which meant that she had plenty of paintings to produce. Gilbert was busy drumming up publicity for it, plus he was planning an independent financial management business that he intended run from home.

'To us.' Gilbert raised his flute with a smile.

'To us!' Holly said, clinking her glass with his.

Gilbert was still gazing at her with an intense look in his eyes. He was beginning to look more chilled out, she thought. She didn't miss his navy suits, perpetually neat hair, beeping phone, distracted eyes and tense jaw of old. Nowadays, small curls nestled at the nape of his neck. He preferred comfy jeans, checked shirts, and chunky knitted jumpers. He even padded around the house barefoot. Holly wasn't used to seeing him like this.

'I love you, Holly,' he said suddenly. 'I'm proud of you.'

She gazed back at him, a little startled at the uncharacteristic display of emotion. As they gazed at each other, she felt a long-forgotten, yet familiar pang.

'Gilbert,' she said impulsively. 'Let's go upstairs.'

If Gilbert couldn't believe his luck, he hid it well. It had been a very long time indeed.

'Sure,' he said lightly, grabbing the champagne bottle. 'I'll lead the way.'

It felt weird but right being intimate with Gilbert once more. After two swift glasses of champagne to fortify her nerves, Holly was soon lost in the moment as Gilbert kissed her. He was gentle and loving.

Afterwards, they lay in bed, naked.

'Are you okay?' Gilbert asked.

Holly grasped his familiar hand.

'I love you, Gilbert,' she said.

Gently he kissed her on the nose, eyelids and lips. 'I love you too, darling. More than you'll ever know.'

GLORIA HYTHE SURVEYED her vegetable garden. As usual, she had planted an early row of lettuces, which looked leafy and ready to eat. A promisingly warm breeze rustled through the trees. She glanced at her watch; the guests would arrive in two hours.

She strolled around the corner, where a large, manicured expanse of lawn was neatly laid with a marquee and about fifty white seats, all decorated with flowers and ribbons. A white banner was tied to a large oak tree nearby and swelled in the breeze. Its gold lettering read:

Will and Gloria Tie the Knot.

Holly popped her head through the veranda door, which overlooked the large back garden. In her hands were some flowers, from which she was about to make some posies. Lucy was already in her pale turquoise flower girl dress, her blonde hair neatly trimmed and brushed.

'Gloria, pale or hot pink rosebuds?' Holly held up one of each. 'I couldn't decide so Michael let me take both.'

'Both!' Gloria said after a moment's consideration. She smiled at Holly, who smiled back.

'Righto then!' Her head disappeared again behind the door, along with Lucy's, who gave a little wave.

Gloria continued on her way around the outside of the house. Off in the distance, a tractor rattled along the rough farm road leading past the house. A dog barked. Then Will and his big, green tractor appeared from behind some trees on the driveway. Gloria could see Sarge perched as usual upon his knee. The large machine clattered to a halt and Sarge leapt to the ground, with Will not far behind. An excited blur of fur whipped around her legs. Gloria smiled to herself. It had been a long time since she had seen Will move so nimbly.

She tapped her little gold wristwatch. 'Your suit is back from the cleaners.'

Will strode towards her with a smile. 'Just had to check

some fences.' He looked her up and down. 'Isn't it bad luck for the groom to see the bride before the wedding?'

Gloria smiled. 'Everything's ready for you, dear. Holly collected your suit and it's hanging in your wardrobe.'

'Thanks love.'

'I'd best be off then.' Gloria patted her freshly styled curls, which were softly pinned back from her face. 'Could you please let Holly and Lucy know to meet me at home in an hour?'

'Sure.' Will nodded.

Gloria hopped into her car, which was parked nearby. With a small, excited spray of gravel, she drove off to get dressed in her wedding gown. It was not strictly a traditional gown. She had chosen one she could wear again on special occasions. Holly had helped her choose it from a local designer. The fitted bodice had small pleats sewn in, and it fell to a smooth, A-line skirt. From creamy silk taffeta folds peeked tiny crystal beads, which sparkled in the light. A turquoise bolero jacket covered her shoulders and upper arms. She felt like a princess wearing the gown, and admired herself in the mirror.

She heard the sound of an engine outside. It must be Holly and Lucy arriving with the flowers. Soon Gilbert would be here. He had offered to be the wedding car driver. Shortly before the ceremony he would arrive to collect them in a Rolls Royce, which was on loan for the day from Tammy's parents.

Deftly Gloria applied a soft pink lipstick and blush, followed by brown mascara—she had no intention of being fashionably late. She would be punctual, a trait she and Holly shared.

Holly stepped through Gloria's front door. Her pale turquoise bridesmaid's dress was cut flatteringly to allow room for her growing bump. In a few months she would give birth to a sibling for Lucy. Lucy was beside herself with excitement at the prospect of being a big sister.

Gloria gazed at Holly. 'You look beautiful,' she said softly. 'You remind me of your mother.'

'You look beautiful, too.' Holly squeezed her arm with a small smile. 'Mum would be happy for you and Dad.'

'Mummy, the flowers,' Lucy said.

As they retrieved them from the car, Gilbert pulled up in the Rolls Royce. He got out, looking grand in his tuxedo. His eyes glowed with pride when he saw Holly and Lucy—his girls. He hadn't seen them for a couple of days because they had been staying with Will to help with the wedding preparations.

'You all look beautiful,' he said, although his gaze was fixed firmly on his wife as he said this. He held open the gleaming car doors. Hopping in, they tucked their dresses safely out of the way.

'Ready?' He grinned at Lucy in the rear-view mirror, who looked both excited and solemn. She took her flower girl duties seriously and handed Gloria's bouquet to her once everyone was settled.

And with that they drove off, the Rolls Royce purring powerfully along the country lanes.

Chapter Nineteen.

PLACING THE FINISHING touches on the green, red and gold table setting, Holly stood back and admired the artfully placed candles and wreaths. She had always liked the flourish of detail. The house was awash with colour and scent, and there were handmade festive decorations, candles and potpourri carefully dotted throughout. Each room smelled different and her favourite scent was that of driftwood; it reminded Holly of when she was a girl in a pink t-shirt, toasting marshmallows on a remote, sandy Cornwall beach, pulling foil-wrapped potatoes from a bonfire, so hot they burnt your fingers and tongue. Her mum and dad had laughed as firelight danced in their eyes, giddy in each other's company. It was Holly's dearest childhood memory of her parents, and for some inexplicable reason it made her want to escape to the Southern Hemisphere where Christmas was in summer and, according to Tammy, there were sandy beaches galore. One of these days she would have to persuade Gilbert to make the trip with her and Lucy. 'Oh yes, and darling little Flynn, too.' She smiled to herself and tweaked the wreath she had assembled earlier.

Creating the perfect Christmas party atmosphere was therapeutic for Holly, who nowadays spent the majority of her time juggling party preparations and their new baby. Gilbert loved to see the different things she created take shape in her hands. He never ceased to marvel at her ingenuity, despite the fact she was sleep deprived because of their new-born son and his somewhat erratic feeding and sleeping hours.

Tammy and Matt would be there for the Christmas party tonight. Aunty Tilda was also joining them from Leeds, and for good measure Gilbert had invited a couple of his old buddies from the City.

Pack your toothbrush, read the red and gold, hand-crafted invitations. Holly had made a miniature cut-out nativity scene for each of them. There were plenty of spare rooms at Larkspur for everybody to sleep over, if required.

Holly enjoyed dressing for the occasion. She had found a beautiful coral-coloured dress on sale at Liberty, which flattered the still-rounded contours of her post-baby body, and teamed it with a pair of gold leather ballet pumps. Her glossy russet hair was curled at the ends with a pair of hot tongs. With natural makeup and a final spritz of peony scent, altogether she presented the glowing image of somebody who was contented and comfortable in her own skin.

Holly's sharp ears detected the sound of an engine and car tyres crunching on gravel outside. Presently, the doorbell rang. It was Tammy, Matt and Aunty Tilda, each bearing gifts. They had travelled together in Tammy's convertible. Holly hugged everybody and quickly invited them inside and out of the biting cold. They all had overnight luggage and Holly wondered how they managed to squeeze everything into Tammy's compact car. Aunty Tilda must surely have taken up at least an extra half of one seat. She was also carrying a bottle of her infamous ginger rum, which, with a smile, she handed to Holly.

Once everybody's luggage was deposited in their rooms, Holly began pouring a round of hot mulled wine. As she picked up the ladle, a little wail came from the baby monitor. There were several of these dotted around the house, which allowed her and Gilbert to keep tabs on Flynn.

'I'll take care of the drinks,' Gilbert offered. Holly smiled as she passed him the ladle for the mulled wine.

Sometime later she reappeared, cradling Flynn in her arms. Gilbert grinned proudly as everybody clustered around and admired him.

'He has your colouring,' Matt remarked to Holly with a smile, gently stroking the downy brown wisps on Flynn's scalp. Holly was pleased to see Matt again, and the corners of his grey eyes crinkled with pleasure at the sight of his tiny godson.

Flynn gazed curiously back at Matt with his dark eyes. Matt tickled his button nose and was rewarded with a gummy smile.

Holly nodded. 'And Lucy has Gilbert's,' she replied with a smile. 'One of each.'

As if on cue, Lucy emerged from her bedroom where she had been sketching some butterflies. Her blonde hair now reached her shoulders—Holly could scarcely believe how fast it had regrown. Matt passed Flynn to Aunty Tilda when he saw Lucy. Lucy shrieked with delight and threw herself in his arms. Matt gave her a bear hug, and she chattered excitedly to him. Holly smiled to herself; nothing much had changed and Lucy still worshipped the ground he walked on.

Meanwhile, Aunty Tilda gazed down at the baby in her arms. Flynn grasped a hold of one of her plump fingers with his chubby fist and gazed up at his kindly godmother. His alert eyes were fixed on the gigantic purple baubles hanging from her earlobes. He reached for them, and she chuckled.

The doorbell rang and Gilbert strode off to answer it. His former banking buddies from the city, Thomas and Charlie, had arrived bearing gifts, overnight luggage and a ubiquitous bottle of expensive wine each. Gilbert greeted them both with a brisk embrace and back-slap. As it happened Thomas's girlfriend couldn't make it, and Charlie had recently split with his wife of three years. Such high-pressure work tended to be conducive to failed marriages, Gilbert observed. He was glad that all those years ago he had elected to settle down with Holly and not one of those gold-diggers who seemed drawn to city bankers like flies. He was pleased his friends could make it tonight. Holly was also curious to meet them—she hadn't met anyone from Gilbert's old line of work before. He had always been far too busy for that.

Tammy's eyes lit up when she spied Gilbert's friends. As usual she was immaculately dressed, wearing a cropped, buttery leather jacket, a slinky red dress and a pair of metallic pumps. Her dark hair was freshly blow-dried, and her lips and fingernails were a shiny red. The younger of the pair, Thomas, looked as if he might be a bit of a devil, Tammy thought. From underneath her heavy fringe she batted her extraordinary eyelashes, and immediately struck up a conversation with him.

Holly looked at Gilbert, who good-naturedly rolled his eyes. After a few moments Tammy grew bored, no doubt on account of all that talk of finance, Holly thought. She watched as Tammy flitted over to Matt. Soon they were talking animatedly, and…what was that look in Tammy's eyes? Wait a minute, did she…fancy Matt? And what was that goofy grin on Matt's face about? Holly's mind raced. It was clear they fancied each other, but just didn't know it yet. Everything was in the right order. They were friends— check. Single—check. Both attracted to each other—that was obvious. She stole another look at them. Tammy's azure blue eyes shone as she listened intently to something fascinating Matt was saying. There was no sign of the exaggerated eyelash batting she usually employed when she flirted. Instead she looked relaxed, natural and, quite frankly, was hanging off Matt's every word. Furthermore, Matt was enjoying the attention. His grey eyes glinted back at her with that goofy grin still plastered to his face.

Holly's mind wandered to her first date with Gilbert. He had taken her for a posh picnic lunch and a countryside drive in his then brand-new Aston Martin. Holly occasionally teased Gilbert about the goofy grin, which had been fixed to his face at the time. It was one of those things, she supposed, when you really fancied someone it could be quite difficult to disguise it. Gilbert still owned that Aston Martin, although more often than not it was parked up in one of the garages. Over the years he'd had little time to drive it, but held onto it nonetheless. Nowadays he hoped to dust off the elegant machine and take it for a few more spins yet, along the pretty country lanes of Surrey, and further afield.

The time came for everybody to exchange gifts. Flynn seemed to greatly appreciate the engraved silver rattle from Matt. Immediately he placed it in his mouth and gave him a gummy, wet grin, as babies do. The knitted bootees with matching beanie and scarf from Aunty Tilda fitted him perfectly. Holly thanked them each with a hug.

Lucy adored the Tiffany starfish necklace from Tammy. 'Thanks, Aunty Tammy,' she said, putting it on immediately. 'I love it.' Her eyes glowed. She looked up to Tammy, and whenever the opportunity arose Tammy would create weird and wonderful hairstyles for her. In fact, Lucy was hoping that tomorrow Tammy would do just that.

Holly didn't know what to say when Gilbert handed her a small, gift-wrapped parcel. She passed Flynn to Matt and carefully removed the wrapping. Inside was a flat jewellery box, which looked antique. With eyes like saucers, she opened it. Nestled inside on the black velvet lining was a stunning diamond pendant on a white gold chain. When she held it up it caught fire from all directions.

Gilbert fastened it around her neck and whispered in her ear as he did so. 'It was my grandmother's, now it's yours. I hope you like it.'

Holly cast her mind back to a time when she would have chastised Gilbert for giving her such a lavish gift. She would have said that time with her and Lucy was worth far more. Thankfully that time had now passed. Instead she smiled and kissed him graciously on the lips.

'Thank you,' she whispered, meeting his gaze.

She was glad she had married Gilbert. Admittedly she had not felt that way one hundred percent of the time, but then again, who did? She was sure that marriage wasn't always meant to be plain sailing. Gilbert was a good man—almost perfect, like her and everybody else, she supposed. The most important thing was that he loved her and treated her well. She had learned that was not something to take for granted.

After all of the presents were unwrapped, Holly took Flynn upstairs to his little cot. He was worn out from all of the attention he had received. Soon, there was a tiny tap at the door. Tammy poked her head through. 'Mind if I join you?'

'Course you can.' Holly waved her in.

Tammy curled up on the cosy rug. 'I wanted to catch up with you before the party gets into full swing. How are you getting on?'

'I'm doing great.' Holly smiled at her friend and touched the diamond pendant at her neck. 'Thanks in no small part to the help I got from everybody.'

Tammy smiled back at her friend in the half-light. 'I'm glad,' she said.

Holly thoughtfully stroked Flynn's little forehead as he drifted off to sleep. 'I don't know what I'd have done if I didn't have someone to talk to. Anyway, how are things with you? I didn't realise you and Matt were so…friendly?'

'I hope you don't mind.' Tammy gazed expectantly at Holly.

Holly contemplated what to say next. 'You seem to have things in common,' she said, and awaited Tammy's reply.

'We do have things in common actually. Turns out we both have French grandmothers. I also can't believe he's single! A guy like him…'

'I think the feeling's mutual,' Holly replied. Flynn eyes were flickering at their muted conversation and Holly continued stroking his soft forehead to settle him.

'Listen, I know I warned you off him a while ago. I'm sorry I did that, it was selfish of me.' Holly hoped she was saying the right thing.

'Don't worry.' Tammy gave a small, rueful laugh. 'I know I'm a notorious flirt and I'm hoping to reform my ways.' She fiddled with a zip on her jacket.

'It's just a phase, I'm sure,' Holly replied. 'Anyway, I love you no matter what.' She put her hand on Tammy's arm and squeezed it lightly. 'I couldn't ask for a better friend than you.' Holly fished in her pocket and handed Tammy a small gift-wrapped box. 'Here. For you.'

Tammy gave her a questioning look as she tore the paper off. She smiled when she saw the silver friendship bracelet nestled inside. 'Thank you,' she said. 'I've been admiring these for ages. Impeccable taste, as always.' Leaning over, she hugged Holly.

Flynn was asleep by now. The girls linked arms as they crept from the room and downstairs towards the party. Matt was deep in conversation with Gilbert and it looked serious. Tammy and Holly exchanged glances and walked over to where they were standing. Gilbert put his arm around Holly's waist when he saw her there.

'I was just explaining to Matt all of the reasons why I don't miss my old job.'

His friends approached and Gilbert grinned. 'Fancy a wee dram of whiskey?'

They agreed.

'I'll join you in a bit,' Matt said.

The three men made their way to the oversize antique drinks cabinet on the other side of the room. Holly watched Gilbert open a bottle of his favourite single malt. She smiled to herself; it had been a long time since she had seen him let his hair down.

Spying Aunty Tilda biting into a Jamaican turkey patty at the buffet table, she decided to leave Tammy and Matt to their conversation.

'What do you think of the patties?'

Aunty Tilda smacked her lips together and brushed a few crumbs from her green and orange patterned tunic. 'Well dear,' she nodded approvingly. 'These are excellent.' She then changed the subject. 'What a beautiful home and family you have. You're blessed with all of this.'

Holly nodded thoughtfully. 'It took me a while to appreciate it.'

Aunty Tilda smiled warmly. 'My dear girl, sometimes we don't appreciate what we have until it's too late. You, on the other hand, didn't throw away the good things you have. You're a survivor.'

Holly took a moment to digest this. 'Thank you. I'm glad you could be here tonight,' she replied.

Aunty Tilda reached for a miniature bacon-wrapped sausage and popped the whole thing into her mouth. 'These are my favourite,' she said.

Holly helped herself to one also, followed again by Aunty Tilda. Until just now, Holly wondered, hadn't the plate been piled high with these tasty meat morsels? Holly's gaze shifted to Aunty Tilda, who winked.

'We all have our crosses to bear,' she said, as if reading her mind.

Holly looked intrigued, not quite understanding what to make of this comment.

Aunty Tilda nodded and daintily wiped her hands on a napkin. 'Well,' she began, 'you can probably guess that being a model all that time ago was torture for someone like me. I got by on fresh air, champagne and coffee. I looked like a stick, but what a fabulous time it was.' She sighed, a breath tinged with bacon and memories. 'I'm making up for lost time.' She deftly posted another sausage into her mouth.

'Were you ever married?' Holly ventured.

'Oh yes, a long time ago.' Her eyes grew a touch misty.

Holly was even more intrigued. 'Can I get you a drink?'

Aunty Tilda nodded. 'Some of that champagne, please. Reminds me of my younger days.'

Holly retrieved a fresh bottle from the fridge and popped it open. She filled two flutes and handed one to Aunty Tilda, who thanked her.

'Now, where were we?'

'My husband…he was the handsomest man you can imagine: skin like sticky toffee, eyes like melted chocolate and hands, well…' Aunty Tilda gave a little shiver. 'He told me he didn't like London, said it was too cold and unfriendly. I didn't listen and he ran off after five years of marriage. Went back home and that was that. Then I was on the heartbreak diet and being a stick suddenly became easy. I could've followed him, but I didn't. I stayed in London with all my fancy fashion friends and kept on living the fast life.'

'Do you know what happened to him?'

'He wanted a divorce, so I gave it to him. Didn't argue. Last I heard he'd remarried and has four kids. I never remarried. He was the love of my life.'

Holly was thrown by this revelation. 'Refill?'

Aunty Tilda nodded and Holly topped up her flute. They sipped companionably.

'You've become an important part of my life, Aunty Tilda.' Holly affectionately squeezed her plump hand. 'Flynn's godmother and my friend.'

Aunty Tilda nodded sagely and smiled. She considered what she was going to say next.

'You know, I made my choices,' she said. 'But I still count my blessings every day. These days I have a good job at the school and I don't have to worry about my figure. I've got friends and family in Leeds, and I'm happy.'

Holly reflected on this. Now there was someone who graciously faced life's knocks, but didn't make a pastime of feeling sorry for themselves. Instead, they counted their blessings. That, she supposed, was a great blessing in itself. She looked around the room. Each face was beaming with good cheer. Matt's grey eyes crinkled at the corners as he laughed at something amusing Tammy was saying.

Gilbert was discussing whiskey with his friends. Holly could tell he was doing this by the way he was holding his glass up to the light and rolling the amber liquid inside. She had always appreciated Gilbert's calm sense of fun and seeing him like this filled her with pleasure. She smiled as she gazed at her husband. They had journeyed to a frighteningly dark place, and together they had found their way towards a more satisfying future as a couple and as a family. Through thick and thin their commitment to each other, when it mattered most, triumphed.

Gilbert must have felt Holly's eyes upon him because he glanced in her direction. A wry smile played across his lips as he watched Thomas suddenly dart away to answer his mobile phone.

Holly shot him a questioning look as if to say, 'So, do you miss all of that?'

Gilbert caught it and grinned. He strolled over and kissed the tip of her nose, gently.

'Not for one second,' he said.

Acknowledgments

I would like to thank all those who helped bring *Almost Perfect* to fruition. Much time, effort and expertise has made this happen, and I am extremely grateful.

I trust I will be forgiven for any inaccuracies regarding the medical and legal practices mentioned in this story. Although these processes were researched, in places creative license may have crept in for the sake of the story (this is a work of fiction after all).

It has been an incredible journey. The friends, family and experts involved have made it a journey worth taking and I couldn't have done it without them.

A Note About the Author

Delia lives in London and keeps a low profile.
She married young and also is very happy with her
almost perfect life.

www.ingramcontent.com/pod-product-compliance
Lightning Source LLC
Chambersburg PA
CBHW021144130626
46554CB00005B/1647